Loving

Summer

kailin gow

Loving Summer (Loving Summer Series #1)

Loving Summer
Published by THE EDGE
THE EDGE is an imprint of Sparklesoup Inc.
Copyright © 2012 Kailin Gow

For information, please contact:
THE EDGE at Sparklesoup
1·252 Culver Dr., A732
Irvine, CA 92604
www.sparklesoup.com
First Edition.
Printed in the United States of America.

ISBN: 978-159748-044-4

Prologue

When I think of my summers spent at Aunt Sookie's Malibu "pad" as she called it, I think about first kisses, first love, and first heartbreak. I think about my friendship with Rachel Donovan and her brothers Nathaniel (Nat) and Drew. I think of all the sunsets, dawns, and first attempts. And then there was this summer, the summer I grew up, in more ways than one, and everyone noticed, especially the boys, especially Nat. – Summer Jones

Rachel Donovan paused at the door to the room her brothers shared, steeling herself for the kind of chaos within. What was it about guys that they couldn't live in any space that wasn't knee deep in unwashed clothes?

Okay, so maybe her own room wasn't exactly perfect, but she was a sixteen-year-old girl. And she was meant to be the rebellious one. It was *allowed.*

She pushed open the door to see Nat and Drew still stuffing clothes into their bags for the summer vacation. Nat was a year older than she and Drew, with short, wavy deep copper hair, an increasingly muscular build, and a good three or four inches in height on either of them. Drew was handsome, built like the athletic star quarterback he was, with jet black hair that would have matched Rachel's except for the purple streaks running through hers, deep blue eyes that did match, and those same high cheekbones. Even though they were only fraternal twins, people always commented on the similarities. But the difference was he was tall, almost six feet, two inches, and muscular, while she was average and not muscular.

The room was every bit as bad as she'd thought it would be. Worse, even, because now there were clothes strewn over the two beds while they tried to work out what to take with them, the rejects joining everything else on the floor. Rachel picked her way through it as she headed inside.

"Aren't you two ready to go to Summer's Aunt Sookie's place yet?"

"What's the rush?" Drew asked. Nat just shrugged.

"What's up with you two?" Rachel demanded. "It's like you don't *want* to spend the summer in a Malibu beach house or something. Is the idea of spending days on the beach that bad?"

Drew shoved a few more clothes into the bag, stuffing them down into it hard. "It is when I have to miss football camp for this."

"Like you and the other jocks don't spend all year running into one another anyway," Rachel shot back.

"This is a big deal for me," Drew pointed out.

Rachel snorted. "Like you aren't a shoo-in for some dumb jock football scholarship anyway. A few weeks at Summer's aunt's place aren't going to hurt. Come on, are *you* really telling me that you'd rather spend the time playing football than on the beach talking to all the girls there?"

"I would if it means you're going to be there in a bathing suit," Drew replied. "There are some sights the world isn't ready for."

Rachel looked around for something to throw at her twin, couldn't find anything suitably heavy looking, and settled for ignoring Drew instead. She turned to Nat. "What about you? What's got you sulking here?"

"I'm not sulking," Nat said. "I'd just rather be here."

"With Chrissy," Drew added from behind Rachel. Nat shot him a dark look.

"Why not?" he demanded. "I've only just hooked up with her, and now I'm supposed to just go off to Malibu?"

Rachel rolled her eyes. "Like you seriously think she won't be here for you when you get back? You two are so into each other it practically makes me want to throw up."

"Isn't that your response to romance generally?" Drew asked.

"This from the guy who seems to be making his way around every girl in our class?"

Her brother shrugged. "Can I help it if they all seem to want me?"

That got another eye roll from Rachel. "Arrogant, much?"

Nat stepped in, the way he always seemed to so that they wouldn't end up fighting. It was no fun being a twin with a sensible older brother, sometimes. "Look, Chrissy and I are not in love, guys. Infatuated right now, yes. I mean we went out a few times but that's about it."

"Did you actually want something, Rachel?" Drew asked. "Or are you just here to make sure that we never finish packing?"

Rachel remembered and pulled out her phone, bringing up the photo that Summer had sent over.

"Summer's aunt is going to be busy at her acting school, so Summer is picking us up herself. She sent over a photo so that we wouldn't miss her at the airport. I'm kind of glad she did. She might have been my best friend, but I haven't seen her in, like, forever. I wouldn't have recognized her."

Nat took the phone.

"She's changed a bit," Rachel said, and as her brothers looked at the photo, she watched for the moment when their expressions said they'd finally realized just how much Summer had changed. The slightly awkward thirteen year old in glasses, with braces and puppy fat was gone in the picture she'd sent, to be replaced by a chestnut haired, blue eyed beauty with a willowy body, delicately tanned skin and a perfect smile.

"Whoa," Drew said.

Nat did not say anything, but his eyes looked pensive.

"It's quite a change, isn't it?" Rachel said with a smile of her own, just to let her brothers know that she'd seen their faces. "Honestly, I'm not even sure if I can be friends with someone *that* pretty. I mean, Summer looks like she can easily be a supermodel, better looking than the queen bee in our school, so she's probably turned into a total bitch."

"Because all pretty girls are mean girls?" Nat laughed. "Looks like you're going to have to get over the stereotype there, Rachel. Anyway, it isn't even true. Chrissy's beautiful, and she's as sweet as anybody you could ever meet."

Rachel took her phone back from him. "Because you're into her right now. We'll see about that in a month." She'd barely gotten her phone back when Drew snatched it from her. "What are you doing?"

"What?" Drew shot back. "I just want to make sure that I recognize her."

"So it has nothing to do with the part where you think she's hot?" Nat asked.

"What if it does?" Drew shrugged. "I've always… I've always thought she was kind of cool."

Rachel gave him a warning look. She knew what her twin brother could be like. "Don't you dare go there," she said. "Summer's one of my best friends. You are not just going to play with her and sleep with her like all the other girls you date. She's off limits, Drew. I mean it."

"You'd better listen," Nat said, with a look that made it clear he wasn't serious. "We wouldn't want to be on Rachel's bad side."

Drew caught his cue neatly. "She has a good side?"

Why was it that her brothers always teamed up on her, Rachel demanded of any part of the universe that was listening? It was meant to be twins who teamed up on the rest of the world, wasn't it?

"I'm serious, Drew," she said. "I don't want Summer getting hurt. Besides, I don't think you're even her type."

"I'm not her type?" Drew said, looking slightly offended. Maybe it was just because he couldn't believe that there was any girl whose type he might not be. "Well, maybe she isn't *my* type. Had you thought of that?"

"She has a pulse, doesn't she?" Nat asked, and was rewarded by Drew throwing one of the t-shirts for Sookie's Acting Academy that Summer had sent over at him.

"He has a point, Drew," Rachel said, moving to sit down on the edge of the bed. "Right now, it seems like you're interested in any pretty girl who looks at you."

"That isn't true," Drew insisted.

Rachel shook her head. "All right then. Any pretty girl who's prepared to sleep with you because you're the star quarterback. You use them and then you leave them, and I don't want Summer hurt like that."

Drew finished shoving clothes into his bag and yanked the zipper shut. "Why are you assuming that it's always my fault?"

"Maybe because it usually is?" Nat suggested. It looked like he'd finished packing too, and he put his bag beside Drew's. There were still plenty of clothes left everywhere. Rachel knew better than to wonder whether they'd do anything about them. "Face it, Drew, you aren't exactly the kind of guy to settle on one girl. How many girlfriends have you had in the last year?"

Drew picked up his bag and grinned the kind of boyish grin that did a lot to explain why he'd worked his way through most of the cheerleading squad. "None. I don't have girlfriends, just girls who like to have their way with me."

Rachel rolled her eyes. "And how many girls are that stupid?"

"IQ has nothing to do with it, little sister by five minutes. When it comes to me, they all think with something else. Believe me, just because I look good without my shirt on, doesn't mean I'm a free for all, which some girls think. It's kind of hard not to be with them when they're practically throwing themselves at me."

"Well then," Rachel said with heavy sarcasm, "the break will do you good. With all those girls making life so hard for you, this will give you a chance to recover."

Not that it made so much as a dent in Drew's ego. He just shrugged. "I guess it would be kind of good to get away. Then, when I get back, the party starts all over again."

Rachel sighed. There wasn't any point even trying when it came to her twin brother, some days. "Yeah, sure. Just finish getting ready, would you?"

"I *am* ready," Drew insisted. He took another look at Rachel's phone, then passed it back to her. "You know, it's going to be good seeing Summer's Aunt Sookie again. *And* that beach house of hers."

"And Summer?" Nat added, obviously trying to stir things up between them.

Drew shrugged. "It's going to be a great vacation any way you look at it."

Rachel headed back to her room, looking for her bag and leaving her brothers behind. Right then, she was kind of thinking that the whole vacation might go a little better if she found a way to abandon them at the airport. It was probably the only way she was going to get any peace, for one thing. But it was too late for that kind of thinking. They were all going, and Drew was right about one thing. It *would* be good to see the old place again.

It would be good to see lots of things. Rachel took another look at the photo Summer had sent her. They'd stayed in touch online, but she hadn't seen her friend face to face since they were both thirteen. Summer was her dearest friend, and she was happy to be seeing her again. She also hoped that Drew would listen to her warnings, because from what she remembered, Summer was fun, and different, and exciting, but also maybe a little too fragile to be treated the way Drew treated girls. She was embarrassed that Drew was the type of walking one-night stand guy their mom had warned her about.

"I hope you know what you're letting yourself in for," Rachel said to the photo, but then shook her head. Summer had always had a crush on Nat, though, ever since she was five years old. No one, no boy had ever been able to shake her out of her crush on Nat, so at least that was a good thing about Drew.

Rachel was looking forward to getting out of the dreary grey San Francisco weather and into sunny Malibu. Aunt Sookie's Malibu pad had always been magical. It was where they could be anyone or anything they wanted. And at this moment, in the Donovans' lives, they wanted to be anywhere other than here.

Chapter 1

Sunsets and First Kisses

<u>Summer</u>

I'm standing by the baggage claim area, waiting for my three friends to arrive, and wondering a little if maybe I should have made one of those large cards with their names sprawled across that people occasionally hold up. It at least keeps me from wondering what it's going to be like when they arrive. Oh God, I don't think I've been this nervous since... well, forever.

The card is out. I don't have one to write on, and anyway, I sent Rachel my picture. I wonder if she was surprised about how much I've changed. I mean, the last time I saw her, I still had my braces in, and boys didn't give me a second glance. She was always the pretty one, even if she did like to hide it.

It's been so *long* since I saw her. Any of them. It used to be that I'd spend practically every day with Rachel, because Aunt Sookie babysat her and the others, or Rachel's mother would look after me while Aunt Sookie was busy with her acting academy. I guess none of us need that now, but we can still surf the way we used to, or go to the beach, or anything. When we all used to stay over at Aunt Sookie's place on the beach every summer, it used to be great.

It's been three years now though. Maybe it won't be so good. Maybe I won't even know Rachel so much. We've talked on the phone and online, but a friend you spend all summer with is different to one you just talk to now and again, right? I haven't seen any of the Donovans since they moved away to San Francisco. And what about Drew? What about *Nat*? I wonder what he thought about the picture I sent. Did he like it? Did he see that I'm not some little girl anymore?

"Summer?"

There's a Goth girl coming towards me, all purple streaked black hair, ivory skin and dark makeup, in a t-shirt and jeans that go with her hair like someone has streaked purple dye on them. I stare at her for a good couple of seconds before I see her face fully and rush forward to hug her.

"Rachel!"

I shouldn't have worried about what it would be like with her back. Just hugging her, I *know*. I know that we're exactly the friends we always were. Okay, so she's done something freaky with her hair, but she's still Rachel. We have *so* much to catch up on. I step back from her just so that I can look at her, and I can see her doing the same. It's like we're re-learning what we look like, or something.

"Wow," Rachel says. "You've grown taller, and you're in great shape."

"Volleyball," I explain. "*Competitive* volleyball. Mom thought it would be great for me to pick up a team sport, so I went for that one."

"You always were better at doing what your mom wanted than me," Rachel says. She smiles while she says it, but she's told me about a lot of it.

"You still aren't seeing eye to eye with her?" I ask. Maybe I should join the diplomatic core after this.

"No, Mom's being a bitch." Rachel's expression darkens, which given the way she looks now is a pretty scary sight. "Ever since she caught Dad screwing around, it's been the same." She shakes her head, and the expression passes, just like that. Maybe it's because it's such a great day no one can stay angry for long. "I don't care, though. I'm here with you, the beach, and Aunt Sookie!"

I hug her tightly again. I've missed Rachel so much. She's like the sister I never had. Talking of siblings...

"Where are Drew and Nat?" I ask with a grin. "You didn't abandon them at the San Francisco airport, did you?"

"I wish. They're here somewhere. There. There they are." Rachel waves over at them and I can't help staring. Drew's grown. He must be over six foot now, and he is chiseled and cut with muscles in all the right places, not really concealed by the plain white t-shirt he wears with his tight blue jeans. He's tanned all over, which makes his blue eyes bluer and his black hair almost blue-black. I remember him as scrawny, maybe cute in a kind of way, but nothing like this. He's now a man with a body and a face that's scorching hot. As for Nat, he's even taller, though maybe not as broadly built as his brother these days. He's leaner, more chiseled, too, which makes his high cheekbones stand out along with his full sensual lips. He's wearing a white t-shirt under a blue and white plaid shirt with loose fitting jeans and boots. They suit him. That deep copper hair of his shines in the sunlight. I can't help staring as the two of them get closer. Almost every female at the baggage claim area couldn't help staring, too.

"Could you maybe not stare at my brothers in open mouthed admiration?" Rachel whispers. "It will only make their egos bigger."

That's hard to do, especially with Nat. Drew... well, he's impressive, and who would have thought that he'd have turned into some kind of gorgeous hunk in just three years, but Nat was my first real boyfriend. My first kiss. I can remember when he used to defend me from the bullies back in kindergarten. He shouldn't be allowed to go around looking like some kind of rock star.

"Summer?" Drew says as they get close. "I'd hardly recognize you if you hadn't sent Rachel that photo."

I can't help looking at him, at how much he's changed. "Three years makes a big difference."

"Nah," Nat says, and his voice is a little deeper than it was. It sounds more self-assured. "You're all still babies compared with me. Good to see you again, Summer."

I glance at Rachel. She knows. She knows exactly how big a crush I've always had on Nat. Okay, so it didn't go anywhere after I kissed him, but I wanted it to. I wanted it to so bad. Just from the way Drew's looking at me, he knows too. About the only one who doesn't seem to is Nat.

Nat throws an arm around my shoulders and I feel myself start to blush. That's just him. Being near him.

"You're taller than you used to be," he says. "I won't have to bend down to talk to you."

Or kiss me, I think, looking at his full lips, but I stop myself from saying it. I manage to make a joke of it. "Oh, come on, I was never that much shorter than you."

"Midget," Nat says simply, his smile widening.

"I was *not* a midget."

Nat raises an eyebrow. "It looked that way from up here. The same as Rachel. The Two Midgets of Malibu."

"It's not our fault if you're just unnaturally tall," Rachel shoots back, and that starts off a brief argument about exactly what kind of height counts as unnatural. I've missed this. I've missed *them*, being part of the Donovans.

"Do you remember the time Aunt Sookie decided to teach Nat to surf?" I say, while they collect their bags.

"Of course I remember it," Rachel says with a wicked smile. From the way Nat looks suddenly uncomfortable, I guess he remembers it too. "He looked like someone had tried to drown him by the time he came in."

"Those waves were big," Nat protests.

"Sure they were," Drew says. "Though mostly not right on the beach."

Pretty soon, they're all talking about the old times we had at the beach house. There were the plays we'd put on right on the beach when we'd spent too much time around Aunt Sookie's Acting Academy, and the beach fires where we'd roast marshmallows, and a dozen other things. Some of them, like playing at being pirates in the surf, were just kids' things. Some of them, like that kiss with Nat, definitely weren't.

"Do you remember the time we decided that a beach house wasn't enough," Rachel asks, "and we ended up camping out on the beach maybe twenty feet from the door?"

I nod. I can remember all of it, from the stars above us then to trying to erect a tent that kept falling down around us through the night. We always had the best time at the beach house when we were kids. It's hard to believe that we've left it so long before doing this again. Will this time live up to it? I smile as I realize it will, because the most important thing is that we're all here. That's what matters.

I lead the way out into the airport parking lot. It's a huge place, and it takes a while to find my car. When we do, the others seem impressed by the huge, shining black expanse of the Grand Cherokee.

"This is yours?" Nat asks like he can't quite believe it.

I shrug. "Mom and Dad want me to be safe out on the road. I guess they thought that an SUV would do it, and Aunt Sookie pitched in to get this one."

"Well, short of a truck, I guess there isn't much bigger than you out there," Rachel says.

"That's the idea." They pile in, and Rachel gets the passenger seat. I'm kind of glad of that. Having Nat beside me would be too much of a distraction as I drive us out of LAX, through the constant traffic that's there on the way out towards Malibu. The beach house is out on Pacific Coast Highway, and we can see the pier from it, with all the surfers gathered nearby, waiting for the waves to be perfect for them. Maybe we'll join them in a while.

Rachel certainly seems excited about that possibility. "I can't wait to get to the beach and into a swimsuit," she says. "Do you know what the temperature was when we left? Sixty degrees. That is not the right temperature for summer. I want to be out on the beach getting tanned."

"There are tanned Goths?" Drew asks. I'd forgotten what it can be like with the two of them, constantly bickering in that way that says they really love one another as deeply as only twins can. It must be nice having brothers and sisters who are that close. In fact, I know how good it can be, because I've had that with them before. Rachel and the boys. I've been that extra sister, as close to any of them as they are to each other. Maybe I'll have that again this summer.

Maybe I'll have other things too. I have to admit, the thought of Nat in board shorts is pretty good.

"We can do that," I say. "We'll get back to the beach house and head straight for the ocean, if you like."

"That does sound pretty good," Drew says. "I don't know how long it's been since I last surfed. I used to love being able to just go out and surf first thing in the morning before breakfast."

"That or running along the beach, while the sun's still coming up," Nat says, and I can picture him doing it. It's only half a memory, because it's not him three years ago that I'm picturing. It's him now, looking gorgeous as he does it.

"So you aren't both ready to rush home to everything back there?" Rachel asks, and I can tell that it's some kind of private joke between the three of them.

"Are you kidding?" Drew asks. "I'd forgotten how good Malibu could be."

I can see Nat in the rearview mirror, and he's smiling. "I think it could be pretty good here," he admits. "Okay, so there are things I'm going to miss about San Francisco, but they'll still be there when I get back."

"And for now, there's the beach," Drew adds.

I can't help laughing at that. I guess when you live somewhere every day you forget just how wonderful it can be. Or maybe you forget just how good some of the other things in the world are, like great friends.

"You know," I say. "I've really missed all of you. I've missed *this*."

Rachel nods. "I've missed it too."

Chapter 2

Thanks to the traffic, it's a while before I can pull up the SUV at Aunt Sookie's place. Her "Malibu Pad" as she always calls it. She got it in the divorce from her first and so far only husband, a producer she married after a wild fling while she was in her twenties. I can imagine Aunt Sookie having a wild fling, though she hasn't gotten married again since then. These days, I think she's mostly too busy with her acting school and the occasional auditions she goes to on the side.

I watch the others looking around at the house, and I wonder what it's going to be like for them, seeing the place for the first time in three years. It's a big place, right on the beach so that it's easy just to walk out through one of the screen doors onto the sand. It's a modern design - I remember Aunt Sookie telling me it was designed by some architect friend of her producer husband…with a large kitchen, a big open plain living area, plenty of guest bedrooms, and a pool out back with a view out onto the beach. There are Oriental rugs on the floor instead of carpets through most of the house.

Somehow, it always feels like home too. Maybe it's just that Mom and Aunt Sookie both have the same taste in décor, going for that Nantucket feel with plenty of whites and blues around the place to reflect the ocean, as well as starfish and shells scattered around the house as ornaments. I know some of them have come a long way, like the multi-colored shell from Japan, because Aunt Sookie occasionally likes to tell me the stories of how she acquired them. It sounds like she had a lot of adventures when she was in her twenties.

My favorite room is that kitchen. It has granite counter tops, and I can remember sitting at them as just a little girl, with Aunt Sookie running through some script or other while she cooked. There's so much space in there. It's the kind of kitchen people don't just cook in, they live in it.

Just stepping into it reminds me of where I am, and I'm at home instantly.

The others find their spots just as quickly. They've been here so many times that they *know* where they're going to be. The first bedroom on the second floor is for Drew and Nat. The one opposite it is for me and Rachel. She's in there already. In fact, by the time I get there, she's already changed into a two piece swimsuit that's as purple as the streaks in her hair.

"Going for a swim?" I ask.

Rachel nods. "I think it's the only way my body is going to believe that I'm really here."

She heads downstairs, to the pool. I go with her, but don't change. I'm not going swimming just yet. Drew's there, and he takes one look as his twin sister jumps into the pool before stripping off his t-shirt and jeans. In seconds, he's down to his boxer shorts and he jumps right in beside Rachel, sending up a spray of water. Yes, I watch. I'm human, after all.

Nat is making himself at home too, going through Aunt Sookie's collection of video games, half of which people she's worked with have done voice acting for. He turns on the TV, which occupies most of one wall, flicking through the channels one by one to try to see if there is anything either of us wants to watch. There isn't, right then.

"You can't be bored already," I say with a smile.

Nat shakes his head. "I'm not. I'm hungry though. How about we go see what Sookie keeps in her fridge?"

"Sure, but you won't like it." I already know what's there. I can almost hear Nat groan with disappointment as he opens the door, revealing rows of vegetables, fruits, and cold pasta.

"Seems like your aunt eats like a bird," Nat says. "Do you want to go with me to the market to pick up some real food for the grill?"

He wants me to go with him? I can't turn down a chance like that to spend some time with Nat. Even if it is just a trip to the market. "Sure. Let me get my purse."

Nat pokes his head out through the screen door to talk to the twins. "Summer and I are going to pick up some groceries. Need anything?"

"Chips and all that good junk stuff Sookie won't let us have when she gets back," Drew says with a grin.

"Yeah, like ice cream and plenty of chocolate syrup and caramel," Rachel adds.

I shake my head. "Aunt Sookie already has that covered."

"Then nuts, sprinkles, chocolate shells, marshmallows… everything we need to create a Kitchen Sink," Rachel says. A Kitchen Sink. I haven't eaten one of those in three years. I'd forgotten how much fun it could be with them around.

I grab my purse and Nat puts his arm around my shoulders again as we step out back. It's easier than walking through the house to the front door. "We'll get everything for a feast. It's about time you and your aunt get a taste of my culinary skills."

In the pool Drew laughs. "Grilling meat isn't much of a culinary skill."

He hauls himself out of the water; his muscles flat and well defined. I spend so much time training for volleyball these days that it's easy to tell myself I'm just taking an interest in another fitness fanatic, but he *does* look gorgeous. Not as gorgeous as Nat, maybe, because there isn't that history with us, but still pretty hot. His presence is hard to ignore, and I find myself taking him in from head to toe.

He throws on his shoes. "If Nat's showing off his 'culinary skills' I'd better go too."

"Like that?" his brother says. "You're wet, bro."

Drew looks across to me and shrugs, those muscles of his moving in complicated ways. "You mind or do I need to change?"

I stare at him, then remember to answer. "A t-shirt would be good."

"You don't mind about the boxers?" Drew asks, and he moves a little closer to me. Is he trying to tease me? His boxers are wet, dripping, and cling to him like a second skin. My mouth nearly drops open. I can feel myself getting ready to blush, but I'm ready with an answer. "I didn't notice them. I'm more interested in the water you're planning on dripping on the rugs while you go through the house."

Drew grabs a towel, and while he's busy drying off, Nat takes my hand. "Come on," he says. "We should get going, or there won't be time to cook."

"Hold on," Drew insists, rushing inside. He comes out in just over a minute wearing jeans and another white t-shirt. Maybe he didn't dry himself that well, but the t-shirt clings to his muscles.

"That was quick," I say.

"With all those one night stands of his," Nat explains, "he had to learn to dress fast. He has to get out of there before a girl can think he might actually care."

I look at Drew and he shrugs again. "They know what they're getting into," he says. "Why complicate things with emotional stuff?"

"You're a pig, you know that?" Rachel calls out from the pool.

"You want to join us, Rachel?" I ask.

She shakes her head, getting out of the pool and heading for a lounge chair near it. "I'm fine here. It's going to be good having some time away from these two."

"Then we should go," Nat says. His hand is still in mine, and it's so gentle and warm there. Compared to his brother, he's a total gentleman.

The three of us drive over to the nearest Trader Joe's and Nat starts picking out food for the grill: corn-fed beef, scallops, fish. He seems to know what he's looking for, and pretty soon, he's filled most of a cart with it. By the time he's done that, Drew has been around the store and comes back with a cart of his own, filled with soda, chips, hot dogs, hot sauce and more, exactly the kind of junk food he said they were going to get.

"Glad you remembered," Nat said.

"Like I'd forget the hot sauce."

While they're doing that, I become aware of two things. The first is just how well the brothers still get along.

It seems three years haven't changed that. The second is that there are two girls around my age, maybe a little older, checking them out. I can't blame them, but they're pretty obvious about it, just watching them and talking in low voices to one another. One, a dark haired girl whose tight clothes do a lot to emphasize the curves she has, even comes over and pushes what looks like a slip of paper into Drew's hand. They both walk off then, giggling.

"What just happened?" I ask.

Nat shakes his head with a smile. "Just the Drew effect. I'll be back in a second. I just need one more ingredient."

He heads off, leaving me with Drew. I look at him. "The Drew effect? Seriously?"

"I get it most places," he says, starting to grin but then stopping himself. "Honestly, it can get pretty annoying."

"Oh, poor Drew," I say. Like pretty girls giving him their number is really a problem.

"I mean it," Drew says. "Think about it. If I was a pretty girl, and guys were constantly coming up to me harassing me, judging me just by my body, that would be a problem. But because I'm a guy, that's somehow okay?"

"So, girls just want your body?" I ask, as innocently as I can. After all, I've stared at him.

"Ever since I got in shape and made the football team...it's been non-stop."

"Why can't you stop it?" I look around, hoping to catch sight of the girls and tell them to leave Drew alone, but they're long gone.

Drew shakes his head. "It's just what guys do. A girl throws herself at you, you go with it."

"Nat doesn't," I point out.

"No, Nat doesn't," Drew agrees. "He never takes a chance. Never does anything. He wouldn't know a good thing if it were standing in front of him."

I'm suddenly, hotly, angry. Drew can't talk about Nat like that. "Nat might not have your body, Drew, but he's considerate, kind... he wouldn't do anything to hurt a girl."

I can feel tears starting to form in my eyes. Why? Why should they?

Drew takes in a slow breath. "Look, I'm just trying to be honest, Summer. I've forgotten what it's like to have a girl around me who only wants to be friends. Except Rachel, every girl my age is suddenly a prospect."

"Well I'm not," I say sharply. "I'm not the kind of girl who could sleep with a guy without it meaning something, the way it works for you, so I guess you have one girl who'll never be anything else. Besides…"

I glance over at where Nat is still hunting for his missing ingredient, his height making him easy to spot.

"You're still into Nat," Drew says, "so even if you were that kind of girl, you wouldn't be into me. Three years, and you still love him? Summer, let him go. He's not ever going to feel that way about you."

"You don't know that," I insist.

"I'm his brother," Drew says. "I know."

Nat comes back, a jar of something in one hand and his cell phone in the other. "I know," he says, "Chrissy, I miss you already. No, don't worry, there's nothing here that could ever make me forget you." Chrissy?

I push the shopping cart away, heading down the ice cream aisle. After this, I'm going to need it.

"I was trying to tell you," Drew says, keeping pace with me. "Nat has a girlfriend."

"He knows how I feel," I insist.

"But he still isn't with you," Drew points out. He puts a hand on the cart, bringing it to a halt. "You need to move on, or this summer is going to be a hard one for all of us."

He leans forward, wiping away that tear from before, and I realize how lucky I am right then. Drew isn't the little boy he was, but he's there for me. Nat will be too, even if it isn't the way I want, and Rachel is the closest friend I've ever had. Maybe that will be enough to deal with the fact that the guy I've cared about all these years wants someone else. Maybe.

.

Chapter 3

By the time Aunt Sookie comes home, Nat is already cooking up a storm in the kitchen, with Drew working hard alongside him to produce the feast that they've promised us. Rachel and I are in there too, watching them rather than helping out, talking about what things have been like at school and how different they are from how they used to be.

"When did you change your hair?" I ask. "*Why* did you change your hair?"

Rachel shrugs. "It was just more... me, I guess. I didn't want to look like everybody else anymore."

"You never looked just like everybody else," I say.

Rachel shakes her head. I don't think she believes me. "What about the volleyball? You're up for the state team?"

Of course, she's been reading the stuff I put up on Facebook. That's what it's for, after all.

"Just the school team at the moment," I say, "but I'm hoping for state."

Aunt Sookie chooses that moment to come home. She's thirty-six now, and to me it always looks like she's just hitting her prime, like being in her thirties has only made her more beautiful. She doesn't always agree, because she thinks that auditions were easier in her twenties, but I think she looks great. There's that long auburn hair that falls almost to her waist, and those cheekbones that I think I got from her. Her eyes are a deep green that always makes me think more of Nat than anyone in our family, so that it sometimes looks like she's more his aunt than mine. Her skin has the tan that anyone who lives in Malibu over the summer acquires, and she always has great taste in clothes. At the moment, she's wearing a white dress that shows off just how in shape she is, and probably has most of the students at her acting academy either jealous or admiring her.

She seems tired though. It's nothing about her appearance. That's perfect, though she seems to be wearing a lot of makeup around her eyes, like she hasn't been sleeping and she wants to cover it up. Where the tiredness shows is when she's greeting Drew, Nat and Rachel. Aunt Sookie hugs them, and talks to them about how much they've grown, but she's so quick to take a seat at the kitchen table. Maybe it's just been an exhausting day.

"Are you okay?" I ask her, reaching out to take her hand.

"I'm fine. Just tired." She smiles back at me. "I don't know how we're going to eat all the food the boys are preparing for us though."

"They'll eat most of it," Rachel assures her. "They eat like total pigs."

"Well, they're growing boys."

Rachel shakes her head. "If Nat grows much more, his head is going to be brushing the ceiling."

"You've grown a lot too," Aunt Sophie says. "I barely recognized you when I walked in. It's hard to think that it's been almost three years since I last had all of you here together, and I guess plenty of things have changed."

"A few," Rachel admits, and I nod. So many things have changed for me too in that time. Yet there are plenty of things that haven't.

"You're all growing up," Aunt Sookie says. "It's kind of sad in one way, because none of you will be interested in my old stories anymore."

"Hey, I remember those," Drew says from where he and Nat are cooking. It looks like they're almost done and they start to lay out plates of food. Rachel and I move to help them. Aunt Sophie stays where she is. It really must have been a long day.

"I remember too," Rachel says. "Wasn't there something about a princess and a pirate?"

"You remember then?" Sookie says. She smiles. "Of course, it's all kids' stuff. Not really the kind of thing you'd want to hear now."

"I think I'd kind of like to hear it again," I say, bringing over a couple of plates piled high with hot dogs, burgers, steaks, and a mixture of all the other stuff we got from the market. It seems that once Nat starts cooking, he doesn't stop.

"I'd like to hear it too," Nat says, taking another seat and smiling. "I remember you telling it lots of times."

To my surprise, Drew and Rachel want to hear it too. I guess it's not for the story, because we all know it's kids' stuff really. The kind of story that you could tell a six or seven year old, because that's how old we were when Aunt Sookie first started telling us it. It's more about remembering those times, like seeing an old photograph, or going back to a place you used to visit.

"Now, it used to be that there was a pirate who lived in Malibu, taking ships from near the coast; raiding up and down it until one day he met a princess when he captured the ship that she was sailing on and ransomed her back to her father the king. But in the time when she'd been a guest on his ship, they'd fallen in love with one another."

Sookie takes a sip of the soda she has in front of her. She hasn't eaten much with it so far, but then, she's been too busy telling her story.

"Now, the king wasn't about to let his daughter marry a pirate, and the pirate couldn't go fetch her from the kingdom's capitol, so they got messages to one another, and the princess arranged to go on a long tour with her servants, letting the pirate know where she would be. Only one of her servants found out, and she arranged for the pirate to get the wrong details about where the princess would be. When the princess wasn't where the pirate thought she would be, he didn't give up though. Instead, he followed her to the ends of the earth, searching for her. Yet when he finally found her, it was here, in his Malibu home. That's why some of the stars above seem to form the shape of a P. For pirate, or princess, or maybe just the perfection of their love."

"I always used to love that story," Rachel says when my aunt is done.

"Me too," Drew admits, and that's a little stranger. I'd have thought that the jock he's grown into wouldn't admit to liking a romantic story like that.

"It brings back lots of memories," Nat says, "but there aren't actually any stars in the shape of a letter P, are there?"

Aunt Sookie shrugs. "Well no, but you didn't know that at the time. As I recall, you spent hours looking for them when I first told you. You always were the inquisitive one. Smart, inquisitive, and usually up to no good."

"I think that part would be Drew," Nat says with a laugh we all join in. Even Drew.

Sitting there like that, with them around me, it's so easy to think back now to the moment we first met. It's so clear that it might have been yesterday, even though it's actually more like ten years. Aunt Sookie couldn't have been more than twenty-five or six then, and looking back, she was so young looking. My mom's five years older than her, so I guess that's where the difference came from, but even so, it seemed almost strange for this young twenty something to be looking after me while my mom worked afternoons in LA.

Yet she wasn't just looking after me. She was looking after three kids who lived near her too. I can remember how nervous I felt, hearing that there were going to be other kids there. I was nervous right up to the point where I saw them. I remember seeing Rachel first, this dark-haired, very pale little girl who looked very sad as she stood there.

"What's wrong?" I asked her, because I didn't want her to look sad. She seemed nice, so she shouldn't be sad. It was the kind of thinking that made sense, when I was six.

"I wish my mom was here," she said. "I miss her."

"I miss mine too," I remember saying. "Maybe we can miss them together."

I remember holding her hand at that point, and deciding that we were going to be friends. I guess I got that part right. I remember that after that, Drew came up to us with popsicles Aunt Sookie gave him to give to us.

"Are we playing a game?" he asked.

"No," I remember replying. "We're missing our mommies together. Because we're friends now."

"Well, I want to be your friend too."

I remember that Nat was the only one who wasn't scared and homesick that day. He was too busy going off exploring the house and the beach, looking around for interesting shells like the ones on Aunt Sookie's shelves. He was also the one who brought about the story, because after a while, when Sookie offered to tell us a story, he was the one who said "Is it a story about a pirate? I like stories about pirates."

"I know you do, and I know that Summer and Rachel like stories with princesses in them, and this one has both."

So she told us the story, but the part I remember most is that she dug around in a huge dress up box, which had to be mostly things taken from her acting school or old movie sets, and she came out with costumes. Nat was the pirate, Drew was some kind of sea monster, Rachel was one of the stars, and I was the princess. I remember her leading us out onto the beach with a big bag of marshmallows and having us act out the story as she told it. I remember Nat made a good pirate, battling sea monsters, travelling around under the stars, searching for his princess.

I remember the part at the end, where the pirate and the princess were meant to kiss. Or pretend to, since it was just a game. And Nat kissed me. He actually kissed me. I smile as I remember how fast I wiped my mouth, and Rachel made fun of it, because obviously her new friend kissing her brother was *hilarious* for her. But I remember that even then I didn't think it was so bad, and that if Nat had been the pirate and I was really the princess, then I wouldn't have gone back to my stupid father the king in the first place.

From the way some of the others around the table look, I guess that they're remembering the same moments. I look over at Nat. He's not looking at me, so it's easier. He was the first boy who ever kissed me, and we've been closer than most people ever get, because we practically grew up together. Yet part of me knows that it doesn't quite work like that. All those great memories are just memories.

Kailin Gow

We can't go back to them, even with Aunt Sookie's stories. Yet I can think about them now. Not just what it was like to kiss Nat when we were both little kids, but what it might be like to kiss him now. Or maybe not. Like Drew said, he's with someone.

Still, I bet he'd look pretty good as a pirate these days.

Chapter 4

The next couple of days are hectic but fun. I'd forgotten what it could be like to have the others around, so that every time I think things might be about to get a little boring, Rachel is there to suggest that we hit the beach together or go to one of the local malls, or Drew is there, offering to go running with me, or Nat is asking me what I have planned for the day. The three of them are constantly doing something, like they're determined to make up for lost time when it comes to this summer.

Then there's the time I spend helping my aunt at her acting academy. I've spent so much time there that it just seems natural that I should help out. When Aunt Sookie needs someone to play opposite her in one of the sessions, why not the niece she's been practicing roles with for years? When she needs someone to help with one of the classes for kids she runs while she's taking a private lesson with someone, why not me? Most of the things we do in those sessions are the kind of thing she had me, Rachel, Drew and Nat doing for fun when we were little kids, and it means that my summer job is a lot cooler than most girls my age have.

Sookie's academy is doing pretty well this summer. Maybe it's all those contacts she has left over from when she was married. Maybe it's that there's something very welcoming about the place, an old theater that was getting shut down before she took it over for her school. Or maybe it's just that Aunt Sookie is good at getting people to act, because a lot of her students seem to find roles in TV or on the stage. Not all of them. Not even most of them, because that's not how it works when so many people want to be actors, but plenty.

There are even a few famous faces around. I've seen Astor Fairway around, apparently taking private lessons in between starring in some new teen sitcom that's going to air later in the year. He's somehow even more good-looking off screen than on it, with short blond hair that seems to spike and curl all at once, big blue eyes that I've seen in close up on TV plenty of times, but are somehow even more arresting in real life, and the kind of body that comes when how you look is a major part of getting roles. I've mostly left him alone when I've seen him though, because I guess he gets enough girls coming up to him and telling him how much they love everything he does.

A few days after Nat, Drew and Rachel show up, one of our neighbors throws a party. Peterson is a friend of Nat's, and for a while the two were pretty much inseparable, so I guess he wants to say welcome back. Maybe it helps that his parents are out of town, too. It's been so long since we've all been to a party together that I can hardly wait for it.

It's as good as I thought it might be, though it's pretty crowded. It turns out that pretty much everyone from school heard it was happening, and none of them were going to say no to a party right on the beach. Though maybe it's good that some of them are there. I see Rachel talking to a boy I know from my class, named Ryan. Ryan's kind of the class Goth, with dark hair shot through with red, a nose stud, and a generally dangerous look that doesn't really work for him because he's such a nice guy.

"So," I say, "you like Ryan?"

Rachel actually looks nervous about it. It looks like she has it bad for him. "What's not to like? He's gorgeous, we like *all* the same bands, and he seems so nice. Sometimes, I meet guys, and they assume that just because I look this way, I want some kind of bad boy. I just hope he's into me too."

"Of course he's going to be into you," I say. "You're perfect for him. He'd be an idiot not to be. Now, why don't you go find him?"

Rachel nods and heads off. She really is into Ryan, then. Good. I want her to be happy, and Ryan's a good guy.

"Looks like your friend is having a good time."

I spin as I recognize the voice and gaze into familiar deep blue eyes. "Astor, what are you doing here?"

This close, he looks even better than he does when he's on the way to his private lessons. I can see why the camera loves him so much. Astor smiles.

"Mostly, I'm dodging fans. I thought a party might be fun, but it's kind of hard when everyone knows who you are. Thankfully, I'm not the only one attracting attention here."

That's true. Drew seems to have attracted a whole bunch of girls to him, so that he's standing at the center of a small huddle of them. When did he turn into a guy who could do that? As I watch, he puts an arm around one of them, whispering something in her ear. She nods, and they leave together. I guess that isn't any of my business.

"So," I say, "if you could have all that attention, why come talk to me?"

"Maybe because you're the prettiest girl in the room?" Astor says. "Besides, I've seen you around Sookie's Acting Academy. You're her niece, right?"

I nod. "I've been helping out there with some of the classes."

"I know," Astor says. "I saw you. You were good in them. Listen, would you like to go for a walk?" He eyes the crowd of girls who were hanging around Drew, but who now seem to be eyeing him. "Maybe somewhere I'm not about to get mobbed? I mean, if you aren't waiting around here for anyone?"

My eyes seek out Nat almost automatically. He's busy talking to Peterson. Rachel is off in a corner with Ryan, and as I watch, they kiss. Drew is... well, wherever he went with that girl.

"Yes," I say, offering him my hand. "I'd like that."

He takes my hand and we head out onto the beach. The stars are out by now, and it's a beautiful night.

"You know," he says, "when you're working at the acting academy, you really seem to connect with all those kids, and it looks like you're having a lot of fun."

"Well, acting *is* fun," I point out. Astor doesn't look so sure. "You don't enjoy it?"

"I do," he says, "but it's kind of hard too. I've been in one hit show, and I'm filming for another, so I don't really get any time off. All my friends are involved in the show, because I don't really get time to visit my old friends, or they don't understand what it's like. There are days when I just want to be *me*, you know?"

I think I understand. "That must be hard. Is that why you've come out here with me? To get away from all that at the party?"

"No, I…" Astor pauses. "I was wondering if you'd like to go out with me one day. Maybe to Disneyland? I know it's kind of a kids' thing, but…"

"I'd like that," I say, cutting him off. It's such a sweet, nice idea. Not the kind of thing I'd expect from some big time actor at all. Besides, he's cute.

Cute enough that when, a little further down the beach, he leans in to kiss me, I don't stop him. It's a slow, gentle kiss, and it's obvious Astor wants the moment to last, because he draws it out a long time before pulling back from me. I smile at him.

"That's…"

Kailin Gow

I stop as I hear a sound from some bushes nearby. Astor stops too, looking around when I do, just in time to see a girl stepping out of them, adjusting her skirt. It's the girl who left the party with Drew. I think I know what's going on, and when I see Drew coming out of the bushes, zipping his jeans, I know for sure.

I can't help the look of disgust that flickers over my face, because Drew shouldn't just use girls like that. He shouldn't. He obviously sees that look, because he steps closer to me.

"Summer..."

"Save it, Drew," I say. "It's not my business."

Astor puts an arm around me protectively, and I can see a bunch of emotions passing over Drew's features. Guilt, anger, sadness. He reaches out to grab my hand.

"Summer, wait, I need to talk to you."

I shake my head. "We were just going back inside to enjoy the rest of the party, Drew. If you want to come along, then do it."

I start to pull away, but his grip on my hand is tight enough that I grimace. "Drew, that hurts."

"Let her go," Astor says.

Drew lets my hand drop. I don't think it's because of Astor, so much as simple shock at having hurt me. "I'm sorry, Summer, but I really need to talk to you. In private."

He says that with a pointed look at Astor. I look at him too and nod my head. "I'll see you inside, Astor."

"Are you sure?" he asks, taking the hand that Drew's squeezing has hurt and kissing it gently. My heart melts at that point. Astor Fairway was kissing my hand like a knight and I was his lady.

"I'll be fine," I assure him, and Astor heads back inside. Drew pulls me back out of sight of the house before he talks.

"Listen, Summer, I know why you're looking at me like that. I know how you feel about me sleeping around and treating girls like they're to be used whenever I want sex."

"Like I said, it isn't my business."

"That's not what your face says," Drew insists. "If you knew what I was going through… did you know that Mom and Dad are getting divorced?"

I shake my head in surprise. "Rachel didn't say." I'm trying to register the news and wrap my head around it. Mr. and Mrs. Donovan are getting a divorce? It is hard to believe because Mrs. Donovan seems to love Mr. Donovan so much. Finally, I say, "I'm sorry…"

"It's why they agreed to us coming here. It gets us out of the way so they can argue as much as they like. Then I've got all the pressure everyone puts on me at school to be the best. To be the star…"

"So you think that you somehow get to have sex with random girls because of that?" I demand.

Drew grins, like it's all some big joke, which makes me a little angry. "There's nothing like it. Though I hear it's even better if it's with someone you actually care about."

He looks at me intently, and after a second, I get it. "No. No way. I am not sleeping with you, Drew. The thought of that is just…"

"Just what?" Drew demands, his grin vanishing. "The thought of me and you is that bad? Or is it just that you'd rather have the TV star? You know that's what he'll want, right? Guys like him are used to girls throwing themselves at them. I'm just more straightforward about it."

"So you're suddenly here to make sure nothing happens to me?" I ask. Like I believe that. "Just like you were when you were warning me off Nat?"

Drew looks uncomfortable. "I just don't want you to get hurt. I thought we were friends?"

"We are friends," I assure him, and I go to hug him, because we're practically family. Drew pulls me into him, holding me tight against him so that I can feel the strength of his muscles under his shirt.

"You smell really good, Summer," Drew whispers against my hair. His arms drift down, resting right on top of my butt. "You feel good, too." His arms tighten around me, and he whispers, "I'm sorry I disappointed you just now, but that's how I relate to girls, and…"

"Hey, Summer? Where are you?" Rachel's voice comes out over the beach, and in just a second or two, I spot her. She spots us too, and she rushes forward, pulling Drew back from me. "Drew, what are you doing? I told you, Summer is off limits."

"Off limits?" I stare at Rachel. "What do you mean?"

"I know what my brother is like," Rachel said, "and I don't want you getting hurt by him, so I told him to leave you alone." She shrugs. "I'm not having him make you another one of his one night stands."

"Rachel," Drew says. "I wouldn't do that to Summer. We were talking."

"Talking, right," Rachel shoots back. "I'm not blind, Drew. Leave her be."

I shake my head. I'm a little angry, and I don't quite know why. I mean, Rachel is just trying to look out for me, right?

"Rachel," I say, "I can handle Drew. Whatever you think of him, I'm not going to sleep with him, and that's that. Come on, I'm heading back inside."

Rachel starts to walk with me, with Drew just behind us. I figure I can at least share the other news.

"You won't believe this, but Astor Fairway asked me on a date."

"He did what?" Rachel's even more excited than I am. She's literally jumping up and down. "That's great."

"I know." I smile over at her, and I catch sight of Drew. He isn't smiling. In fact, he looks furious.

Chapter 5

I meet Astor at Disneyland, by the main gate. It's been a while since I've been here, maybe because I thought I was getting a bit old for the whole Disney thing, but standing there with him, I just *know* that we're going to have a great day. I mean, I'm going around one of the world's biggest theme parks with Astor Fairway! Even if I were just going for a walk on the beach with him, the way we did the other night, that would be great. Going here with him is going to be something else.

I've kind of dressed up for the occasion. At least, Rachel and I spent the better part of an hour picking out exactly the right sundress to go in. She was so excited for me that anyone would have thought I was meeting royalty. Though as she pointed out, Astor is *TV* royalty.

He looks great today, wearing a hooded top I guess so that he can be less conspicuous if he wants to, over lightly faded jeans. It's such a casual look that he shouldn't look so gorgeous in it, but I get the feeling Astor would look great wearing just about anything.

"Why Disneyland?" I ask, as we step out through the main entrance.

Astor looks at me with a worried expression, like he thinks he might have done something wrong. "If you want to go somewhere else…"

I shake my head. "No, it's great. I used to come here with my aunt when I was younger. It's just… well, I wouldn't have thought it would be your thing."

"Why not?" Astor asks with a smile. "I've always liked it here. It's just fun. It's not trying to be anything else. There's something kind of simple about that, and most of the rest of my life is pretty complicated."

"So you've been here before?" I ask.

"It's been a while since I've been here," Astor says. "Not since I did some filming with them as a kid. But they kind of remember me. I don't think we'll have to wait in line too much."

I hadn't thought of that. Of course they're going to know him here. People know him everywhere. Even while we stand there, I see a few girls looking at him, obviously trying to decide if it's really him, or if they can bring themselves to come up and start a conversation, especially since he's with me.

"You get used to the staring," he says.

I look at him. "Do you? I mean, I don't think *I'd* ever get used to it."

"You must have people staring at you all the time," Astor replies with a smile. "Boys, at least."

I can feel myself starting to blush. "Nothing like that."

Astor shakes his head. "I find that hard to believe. Are you really telling me that boys aren't falling over themselves to ask you out?"

I find myself thinking of Nat, and the way he's never seemed to notice me the way that I want him to. "No, not really. So, what are we going to do here?"

"That's a good question. What are we going to do, Astor?"

I turn around at the sound of Drew's voice. He's there, dressed casually in jeans and a dark t-shirt, looking at me expectantly. Despite my surprise and dismay, I have to admit, he looks hot.

"Drew," I say, "what are you doing here?"

He smiles. "I heard Rachel talking about this place and I realized that I hadn't been here in years, so I wanted to come by. Then I saw the two of you and I thought I'd come over to say hi."

Do I believe that? I don't know what else to think. I mean, why else would Drew be here?

"Well, that's nice," I say. "You met Astor at the party, didn't you?"

"Sure," Drew says, holding out a hand to Astor. Astor shakes it, and I can see the two looking at one another. There's something there I'm not sure I like, like they're in some kind of competition, rather than just two boys meeting.

"Say, Summer," Drew says, "how about if I tag along with the two of you? I bet between us, we can remember all the best places to go here."

I want to shake my head, because the last thing I want is Drew in the middle of my day with Astor, but it isn't like I can exactly turn him away either. I mean, he's one of my closest friends, and we're staying in the same house. I look over at Astor.

"It's fine," Astor says. I guess he thinks he can't really say anything else. "Let's get going."

So we start to look around, and sure enough Drew does seem to remember plenty of the best places to go. At least, he's constantly making suggestions about which rides we should go on, or where we should head next. I have to admit it's pretty fun being there. There are so many things to see and do that weren't there the last time I came. We head over to Paradise Pier, and then to the Hollywood Pictures Backlot, making our way through the crowds and tagging onto the end of a tour when Drew suggests it. Astor keeps the hood of his top up for most of that one, because obviously, if anyone is going to recognize him…

"Hey, Astor," Drew says halfway through, loud enough that everyone else in the tour group hears it. "Have you ever done any filming here? I guess you must have, with some of the shows you've been in. What was the last one?"

"Astor?" a girl in the group says. "Astor Fairway?"

From there, it's a feeding frenzy, because obviously everyone assumes that it's just a part of the tour, and Astor can't walk away without looking like some kind of spoiled, ungrateful superstar. So he has to stand there signing autographs and letting people take pictures with him for close to twenty minutes. People just seem to assume that he's going to do it, and don't seem to think that he might have been there to just enjoy the day like them. They certainly ignore the fact that I'm there with him. One of the girls there even makes a move to kiss him until Astor steps back, laughing, and points out that they haven't even met properly yet. It's such a gentle letdown, when there's a part of me that wants to walk over there and pull her off him physically. But I'm not going to do that, because I know Astor can handle it. Instead, I go over to Drew.

"What was that about?" I ask.

"What was what about?" he says, like he hasn't done anything.

"You deliberately drew attention to who Astor was. Did you want this to happen?"

Drew shrugs. "I didn't know it was meant to be some kind of big secret. You notice that he's completely forgotten about you, Summer? He's too busy dealing with his 'public'."

"And if he ignored them, you'd probably say he was some kind of jerk for doing that," I snap back. "What's wrong with you, Drew?"

"There's nothing wrong with me," he insists. "I'm just here to have a good time. I thought we all were."

"And how good a time do you think Astor is having in the middle of a mob of fans?" I ask.

That gets another shrug from Drew. "You think he doesn't love it really? All that attention? All those girls trying to get as close to him as possible. I'm surprised he didn't let that one who wanted to kiss him do it."

I glare at him. "That might be what *you* would have done, but that doesn't mean he would."

"*Any* guy would," Drew argues. "Honestly, Summer, don't be so naïve. That's what guys do. If you think Astor Fairway is going to be any different, then you're fooling yourself."

"Or maybe you're the one fooling himself," I shoot back. "Maybe you want to believe that every other guy is just like you, because that means that you don't have to worry about the way you are."

Drew laughs. "I don't need to worry, Summer. Now, come on, do you want to get something to eat? It looks like Astor's going to be there for a while yet."

I shake my head. I've had enough of waiting, and I guess that Astor doesn't like being stuck in the middle of the crowd anyway, so I start to push my way through it. I figure that if he tells them to leave him alone, that's him looking like a jerk, but if I do it… well, I'm not a famous actor. I don't care what they think of me. I hook my arm through Astor's, looking over at him and pitching my voice loud enough for everyone else to hear.

"Hey, Astor," I say. "When you're done here, can we go get something to eat, the way we were going to before? I know you'd sign autographs all day, but I'm hungry."

He smiles his thanks as most of the crowd take the hint, letting the tour guide move them along the tour, and letting me pull him away from them.

"Thanks," he says. "I never know what to do when that happens. I mean, they only want my autograph because they like what I'm doing, and it's kind of flattering, but when there are so many people…"

"I can't imagine," I reply. I'm still holding onto his arm. That close, I can smell the warm, clean scent of him.

He smiles. "Would you actually like to go get something to eat? It must be nearly lunch."

"I don't know about the two of you," Drew says, "but I'm starving."

I might not have been prepared to say it before, but after what he's just pulled, it's easy now. "Actually, Drew, I was kind of hoping that maybe me and Astor could have some time alone together."

"You want me to go?" He sounds surprised by that. Surprised, and a little hurt.

"Well, you were originally planning to come here alone, right?" I know that isn't true, but he can't really deny it now, and I do want some time with Astor. "How about if I meet you back at the main gate afterwards, and we can head back together."

"I guess so," Drew says. He obviously isn't happy about it though as he heads off into the crowds around us.

Astor puts an arm around me. "I'm kind of glad you did that," he says. "Not that I mind having Drew around, but I'd rather have you to myself today."

I like the sensation of him close to me like that. "How about if we make a deal then?"

"What kind of deal?"

"I'll keep us away from Drew for the rest of the day so that we can have it to ourselves, if you promise that we can run the next time a group of girls recognizes you."

Astor laughs at that, holding me tighter. "I think I can agree to that. Now, where shall we go get lunch?"

I realize that I don't care. Right then, it doesn't matter where we go next, or what we grab to eat once we get there, so long as I'm with Astor while we do.

We finally meet up with Drew by the main gate a couple of hours later. He's with a girl. He must have met her in the park. She's pretty, in an obvious kind of way, with long red hair, a dress cut low to show off as much as possible, and her arm wrapped around Drew as they sit on a bench by the entrance. Drew's hand is on her thigh, and it looks like he's nibbling her ear.

I've just spent the day with Astor, and Drew annoyed me by trying to spoil it, so why do I care so much about that? Why do I feel like I need to push her out of the way and take that spot next to Drew? Why does part of me wonder what it would be like to feel his lips on my ear like that?

I don't know, but suddenly I want to go home to the beach house.

Chapter 6

❦

<u>Drew</u>

I wake up early to run on the beach, getting dressed in running shorts and an old t-shirt while the sun is still coming up, then heading out onto the sand to stretch and run. I run slowly at first, then quicker as my muscles get used to it, mixing sprints in with slower stretches as I feel like it.

I've been doing this since I got here. Since I first saw Summer. If I run hard enough, and fast enough, then maybe I won't think about her for a little while. Ever since Rachel showed me that photo of her on her phone, I've been thinking about her. She's more beautiful than any of the girls I've been with, and I can't help thinking about what she would be like. What we would be like.

I run with the heat of the morning sun on my back, kicking up sand with every step. There are other people out on the beach, the serious surfers and a few other runners, moving past as they concentrate on whatever is in their own heads. A few of them are women and I watch them as they pass, then hate myself for watching them, because they aren't Summer.

It isn't just something physical with Summer. It isn't just the thought of how good-looking she is, how athletic. It isn't just the thought that if I'd never met her before, I'd still want to be with her more than anything. It's the fact that she's *Summer*. Just thinking about her makes the day better. Just thinking about the fact that I can't have her makes it worse. She's so much more than any other girl.

We've spent so much time together. When we were kids, she was always playing videogames with me and Nat, playing volleyball out on the beach or just being there. She was always running around with us, and she could always run as fast as we could. I know her the way I don't know many girls. With most of them, it never goes deeper than each of us seeing something we like, just the physical.

Not that I don't see plenty I like with Summer too.

I'm starting to breathe just a little harder now as I get warm. I've always liked running. It's just so simple. I run along the edge of the surf for a while, liking the feel of the water spraying around my ankles. None of it gets rid of thoughts of Summer.

Not that she'll be thinking of me. If it isn't Astor Fairway she's thinking about, then it will be Nat. It was always Nat when we were kids. Summer used to follow him around like a lost puppy, but did Nat care? He wouldn't be with Chrissy if he did, so why is she still going after him? Summer has pretty much offered up her heart on a platter, and Nat hasn't even noticed. It kills me to see her like that, when she could be with someone who would appreciate her the way she deserves.

Someone like me. I run past a group of girls settling down for a day at the beach and I barely even glance at them. I'm too busy thinking about Summer. I know how she feels with Nat, because I feel the same way with her. I'm the brother she never notices. I always was. Either she was too busy trying to get Nat's attention to take me seriously, or she was hanging out with Rachel. I thought that maybe now I'm in better shape, I'd get her attention. It's normally enough for most girls. They see me and they see the muscles. They see the football player. That's enough for them.

Not for Summer. If she'd just give me a chance…

What would I do? I pause on the sand, looking out over the ocean at the shifting waves. What *wouldn't* I do? I'd move to LA if I thought I had a chance with her. I'd go to college here, and for football… I'd even risk that if it meant that I could be with Summer. She's what matters.

But I know right now it just isn't going to happen. Even Rachel doesn't want me with her. She thinks that I just want some one night stand with Summer. She thinks that I'm going to hurt her, or ruin their friendship, or something. If I even look like I'm going near Summer, she'll probably find something to do that will make me wish I hadn't. Though apparently, she can do what she likes with that Ryan guy.

Did I do the wrong thing with Astor Fairway? No. I just didn't want him sweeping Summer off her feet and using her. She shouldn't have to deal with guys like him. Anyway, he isn't that good-looking. He isn't as buff as I am, and what kind of name is that? He sounds like a golf course outside a hotel.

I hear someone running towards me along the beach. I guess it's probably one of the girls I passed and I turn with a smile. Then I see who it is and my smile widens. Summer is dressed in a grey, long-sleeve shirt and black jogging pants, with her hair tied back in a ponytail while she runs. She looks amazing, even like that. I don't think there's any way she could ever look less than perfect.

"Hi Drew."

"Hi Summer. Did you enjoy Disneyland yesterday?" With Astor. Without me there. I don't say it, but I want to.

"It was great," Summer says, and when she smiles, it's like the world lights up. "Astor is so considerate and sweet. You saw how he was with all those fans, and with him afterwards, it was great." She pauses, while I wish I hadn't asked. "Did you have fun with that girl?"

"What girl?" It takes me a second to remember that there are girls other than her. "Oh, yeah. She joined me after we went on Space Mountain together. We kind of hit it off."

Summer laughs then. "I bet you did, Drew. I could see you were getting along."

She saw all that? Why does that keep happening to me? "It didn't mean anything," I say as quickly as I can. "She doesn't mean anything. I can't even remember her name."

"I wonder if she feels the same way," Summer says. "I mean, is you not being able to remember her name meant to be a good thing?"

Why is she angry now? "She knew it was just a one-time thing."

Summer's mouth drops open. "A one-time thing? You *slept* with her? In Disneyland? That is just wrong on so many levels. How did you even manage it? *Where* did you manage it?"

I can't help smiling at that. "You'd be surprised how many places you can find where you won't be disturbed when you really want to."

Summer throws up her hands. What? What did she expect? It isn't like anyone is getting hurt. "Incredible. Drew, you really are a girl's worst nightmare. I mean, you look great. You have this amazing body and your eyes are such a dreamy blue, but you behave like a total jerk."

"I think I liked it better when you were saying how great my eyes are," I say. I don't want Summer thinking I'm a jerk. Anyway, why should she care? She's already made it clear that it isn't me she's interested in. If she were, then I'd stop even looking at other girls, but until she is, what I do with them is my business. I can't help it if they all feel that way about me, or if I want to have a little fun.

"What do you want me to say?" Summer asks. "That they're kind of stormy, like the sea? They're not quite as blue as Rachel's, but it's more kind of an intense look. I like that. I like that a lot."

"So there's one part of me you like, at least."

Summer moves close to me, close enough that I could almost reach out and pull her into a kiss. "I like all of you, Drew. I just don't like some of the things you do."

I almost do it then. I almost kiss her, but I know I can't. She doesn't want me, and kissing her will just ruin the friendship that we have. I can't be anything to her other than her best friend's brother, and if I try, I won't even be that close. Summer will push me away, and I'll never be this close to her again. I think for a second or two that Summer will do this for me; that she'll kiss me and I won't have to choose, but she doesn't. Maybe it's better that she doesn't. I'm better off with other girls. Girls who don't want more from me than one night.

I wish I could believe that as Summer pulls back from me. I can feel the heat that's there between us, but I don't dare do anything about it. Not now. Not when she won't close that gap either.

"Are you out here to run?" Summer asks.

I nod. "I've been running every morning since we got here. I need to keep in shape."

"Then I'll run with you," she offers, and sets off down the beach. For a moment or two, all I can do is watch her running, then I set off after her. I think it will be easy to catch up to her, but Summer is even faster than she used to be, staying a little ahead of me for quite a while before I draw level with her and then keeping up the pace as we run along the sand. What do we look like, running together? It must be pretty good, because almost everyone we pass watches us as we run.

Eventually, when we're both sweating with the exertion, Summer turns for home.

"You're done already?" I joke, even though I'm just as tired as she is.

Loving Summer (Loving Summer Series #1)

"Breakfast is nearly ready," she says. "That's why I came out to get you in the first place. If we don't turn back now, we're going to miss it completely."

She starts to run back to the beach house and I follow in her stride. I could keep pace with her, but for now, I want to watch her as she runs. I want to watch every movement of her body as she almost glides across the sand. It occurs to me then that I've spent so long chasing after her, not quite catching her. I want more than that. I *need* more than that. Like the moment before we started running, when I thought we might kiss. It feels like my whole life has been that moment. I've gotten plenty of things. Plenty of girls. But never her.

I chase on after her along the Malibu beach and I know that I can't leave things like this any longer. I don't want Summer to be the girl who might have been. I don't care if that makes things difficult. I don't care if Rachel will *kill* me for it. I'm not going to miss this chance. I'm going to do whatever I have to do to be with her.

Chapter 7

Summer

The day after I first run with him, Drew wakes me up with a knock at my bedroom door. I quickly get dressed and go see what he wants, noticing that he's in his running gear again.

"What is it, Drew?" Rachel moans from her bed. "Can't you see that some of us are trying to sleep?"

"Then go *back* to sleep," Drew suggests. "It's Summer I want to talk to."

Rachel looks at him from her bed, and I can tell it's a warning look, but she doesn't say anything. She's obviously decided to believe me when I say that I can handle Drew.

"What do you want, Drew?" I ask. "You're going to wake Aunt Sookie up."

"I don't want to do that," he says. "I just thought that you might like to come for a run again this morning."

"Are you still obsessing over not falling behind with football training?" Rachel asks.

"I'm just trying to stay in shape," he shoots back. "So how about it, Summer?"

"Well, I do like to run," I say. "I have to keep in good condition for volleyball."

"And it can get pretty boring, running alone," Drew points out.

I nod. "I guess so."

"Great," Rachel says, pulling the covers up over herself. "Go run. Just do it quietly, so I can go back to sleep."

I smile at that and nod to Drew, who goes to wait for me downstairs while I change into my running gear and tie my hair back. Rachel is already snoring by the time I go to run with her brother.

Like he said, it's far better running with him than it would be alone. I still have the sensation of the breeze on my skin and the sun on my face. I still have the soft sand giving way beneath my feet or the harder sand making it easier to run. There are still all the morning people out on the beach, used to me by now in the case of a few of the regulars. It's just that with Drew there with me, I have someone to keep me going and to push me on, so that I run harder than I would have alone.

It's good having someone to talk to, too.

"I'm a little worried about Aunt Sookie," I say when we're about where we turned for home yesterday. "Ever since coming back to the Pad this summer, I noticed she's been tired constantly, and the least little thing seems to take it out of her."

"Maybe she's just a little sick," Drew suggests, slowing down a little. "Maybe she's just caught a bad cold, or something."

"This feels like more than a little," I say, and I can't keep the worry out of my voice. "Like the way she's eating. Suddenly, it's like she's changed her whole diet."

"She has lost a lot of weight since I last saw her three years ago. Well, maybe that's it," Drew says, finally stopping and looking out at the ocean. "Maybe it's what she's eating."

"Maybe." I'm still not convinced by that. It's true Aunt Sookie had lost a lot of weight from when we were kids showing up here every summer, and she's changed her sugar-laden high calories diet to all grains, fruits, and vegetables.

"Whatever it is, your aunt's tough," Drew assures me. "And you'll be there for her. We all will. Now come on. Let's get back and see if my sister is out of bed yet."

We run together most days after that. Sometimes, Drew wakes me up to do it, but mostly, I'm looking forward to it. There's something simple about running with him along the beach, and it's like I get to see the real Drew there too. He's so much more straightforward than I remember, plus he's funny, and cute, and he runs like he wants to push himself to the limit all the time.

Plus, it's like he's going out of his way to be nice to me. Maybe it's all the times that I've caught him messing around with girls, or maybe it's just that he wants to show me another side to him, but he starts doing small things that are just so much nicer than I expect. Most days, for example, he makes me breakfast when I get back, and whether it's pancakes or bacon or something else, he always seems to guess exactly what I'm in the mood for. A couple of times, I don't even have to ask. He just gets the food ready, puts it down in front of me, and I realize that it's just what I want.

Then there are other things. One morning, he brings me a flower, a sprig of purple lupines.

"Where did you get those?" I ask.

"They're down on the beach," he says. "Come on. I'll show you when we run."

He does, and we spend our run heading out to this spot on the beachfront where the flowers grow wild. It's beautiful, with the sun and the beach in the background. A perfect kind of spot to stop and catch our breath before we head back.

This new side of Drew isn't just limited to our morning runs though. A couple of times, he comes with me to Aunt Sookie's academy, and he helps me out with one of the classes for kids. He's a lot of fun there, and he seems to genuinely enjoy it.

"What can I say?" he says when I ask him back at the beach house about it. "I just know how to get along with kids."

Rachel, who's sitting at the kitchen table, snorts. "Mostly because you never grew up."

I see less of Nat than of them in those few days. He's often out with old friends, or going to places he used to go to, or on the phone to Chrissy. He's still around though, in the background, and I still find my eyes going over to him from time to time. Occasionally, I find his eyes on me, but when I look over, he's doing something else. He, Drew and Rachel all do a lot to help out Aunt Sookie, though in different ways. Nat does a lot of the cooking for dinner, while Rachel does more in the way of running errands.

When she's not doing that, she spends a lot of her time with Ryan, though we have plenty of fun too. I get her involved in a couple of games of volleyball out on the beach, and we have a lot of fun, even though Rachel can't really keep up. We go swimming together, and meet up with a few friends she hasn't seen since she moved away. Most of them are a little shocked by her new look, but they quickly realize it's still the same old Rachel under the surface.

And there's Astor, too. Rachel wants details of what happened at Disneyland, of course, and she goes all gooey when she hears how calmly he dealt with all those fans. She also promises to never speak to Drew again if he tries anything else like that. Though I suspect Drew will just smile and say it might be worth it if he hears that threat. Rachel also demands more straightforward details.

"Did you kiss him?"

I nod.

"You actually kissed Astor Fairway?"

"Well, he kissed me, really," I say, and for an instant, Rachel looks completely envious. Then she jumps up and down with excitement again.

"That's even *better!*" she declares.

"How does it make a difference whether he kissed me or I kissed him?" I ask.

Rachel looks at me like she's amazed I don't get it. "Anyone could kiss Astor Fairway. I mean, *I* could. All I'd have to do would be to just run up to him and do it... not that I would," she adds hastily. "I'm just saying that someone could, if she wanted."

"Why does it sound like you've been forming plans for exactly that?" I ask.

Rachel looks shocked. "I would *never* do that. I'm with Ryan, so why would I even want to? I'm just saying that there are plenty of girls who would. So it means more if he likes you enough that *he* kissed *you.*"

That actually makes a weird kind of sense, which suggests I've been spending too much time out in the sun with Rachel today. I shake my head. "Don't make too big a deal out of it though," I say. "I don't know if it will happen again. I mean, we had fun, but there must be lots of hot actresses trying to catch his eye. And they probably won't have Drew showing up in the middle of their dates."

To my surprise though, what happened on our date doesn't put Astor off. He's waiting to talk to me when I next go into Aunt Sookie's academy, and again when I'm done helping with the classes. I guess that kind of shows he isn't the spoiled star Drew makes him out to be, because if he were only interested in me for one thing, he'd have moved on when it didn't go perfectly the first time. He comes by pretty often, sometimes coming back for dinner after he's done for the day with his private lessons with Aunt Sookie.

The first time he does that, it's Rachel who answers the door. She must have seen him at the party, but you would have thought that she hadn't actually spoken to him yet.

"Oh. My. God. Astor Fairway." She looks from him to me, to Aunt Sookie. "You're actually bringing *Astor Fairway* home for dinner?"

"If we can get through the door," Aunt Sookie says gently.

"It's all right," Astor says. He holds out a hand. "Hi. You're Rachel, right? Summer's best friend?"

Rachel shakes his hand and then looks at her hand. "I just shook Astor Fairway's hand. I…"

"Rachel," I say, taking her back inside and letting the others past. "Will you try to maybe not act like a total fan for a moment?"

"I'm not, am I?" Rachel asks, and then stops herself. "I am, aren't I? Oh, Summer, I'm sorry. It's just that he's so totally hot, and… not as hot as Ryan, obviously."

"Obviously," I say, trying to keep a straight face. For me, Astor's far better looking than Rachel's new boyfriend, but Ryan's kind of sweet, and I know she really cares about him, because most of the time Rachel doesn't spend with me, she spends with him. "And I know you're excited. Just, could you maybe tone it down a little? When you get to know Astor, you'll see he's just a regular guy."

"A really hot regular guy," Rachel points out.

"I thought he wasn't as hot as Ryan?" I say with a smile.

"What? Just because he's totally wrong for me that doesn't mean he isn't hot. *And* he must be *totally* into you, or he wouldn't be here."

I shrug. "I hope so. Assuming that *someone* doesn't spoil it by making him think all my friends are crazy."

Rachel bites her lip. "I'll try to be normal. I promise."

I laugh. "You don't have to go that far. Just be yourself."

"Hey!"

Thankfully, Rachel does manage something approaching normal conversation with Astor. She even apologizes for being so star struck. Astor doesn't seem to mind anyway, and after dinner we go out onto the beach together.

"I hope Rachel didn't scare you off from coming here too much," I say.

Astor kisses me, quickly and softly. "Nothing could do that while you're here, and Rachel isn't too bad. She must be a good friend."

"She is," I say.

"It must be nice, being that close to someone."

I remember then what Astor said at Disneyland. All his friends are professional friends. He'll know them through his show, and that will be it. I put my hand in his.

"It is nice," I say. "But you don't have to be alone, you know. Whatever happens, I want to know the real you. All of you."

"I know," Astor says, pulling me to him and kissing me softly. In that moment he looks so happy.

Chapter 8

It's a couple of days later, and Astor has come around again. We stay inside for dinner, but then retreat out onto the porch by the pool to talk. Well… maybe we start out meaning to talk, but pretty soon we're making out. Either is good. Particularly with the way Astor kisses. He's so delicate about it, but at the same time he's very much the one taking charge as his lips explore mine and his hands drift down my back. It's a combination that's hard to resist.

"Why don't you come out to my house in the Canyons?" he suggests.

"You're inviting me to your place?"

Astor smiles. "Well, I've spent so much time at yours, it only seems fair to return the favor."

"Right now?" I shake my head. "I don't think I can go just like that…"

Loving Summer (Loving Summer Series #1)

Astor brushes a hand down the line of my cheek. It's such a soft movement, and a sensual one. "Tomorrow then. I'll come by and pick you up once you're done at the acting academy."

I nod automatically. Astor wants me to go see his place in the Canyons? How can I turn him down? "I'd love that."

Rachel loves the idea almost as much as I do the next morning, and she insists on taking me shopping for something to wear. Apparently, I can't just go to Astor's house wearing any of my normal clothes. We have to find something special. Actually, I don't mind that. It's a good opportunity to spend more time with Rachel while doing something other than staying on the beach.

The main trick is keeping her out of the boutique Goth clothing stores long enough for us to shop for something I might wear. Though we do spend some time in one, while I try to think of things to say about the clothes she picks out other than "It's very... um, black." Actually, now that I'm used to this new look of hers, I actually find myself thinking that it kind of suits her, and we quickly pick out a couple of skirts and tops for her that work.

Then it's my turn. Finding the right thing to wear to Astor's place is tricky, because Rachel is determined that I won't go in anything that is less than perfect.

"I thought you were over the whole fan-girl thing?" I point out, when she rejects my fifth choice of outfit on the grounds that it isn't great enough. "I don't have to dress up just because it's Astor."

"No," she says, "you have to dress up because he's invited you to his house and that's a big deal. You're going to look perfect for this if we have to shop all day, Summer."

"Not *all* day," I point out. "I have to help out with an afternoon class that starts in… um, I think we'd better start to wrap this up, or I'm going to be late."

"Just one more dress?" Rachel suggests. "I think I see the perfect one."

Perfect for her or for me? Except that, when she comes back with the one she has in mind, it *is* perfect. It's a peach mini-dress cut low both front and back, and Rachel has brought back silver heels too, so that the combination is almost dazzling.

"This dress and shoes would show off your long legs and flawless skin. Lots of it! I hope Astor knows how lucky he is," Rachel says, "because you're going to look *great* in this."

I know as soon as I see it that it's the outfit for tonight, which is probably a good thing, because as soon as I have paid for it, I have to run for my SUV so that I can make it to the class I'm helping with.

That class seems to drag out forever. Normally, I'm really into what I'm doing at Aunt Sookie's school, so the time just flies by. Now though, I'm busy thinking about Astor, and the time we're going to spend together, so that the class can't end soon enough. Almost as soon as it is over, I rush back to the beach house to get changed for when Astor shows up. The dress looks every bit as great on me as I knew it would. It's the perfect choice for tonight.

I hear a knock at the door- Astor's here already?- and rush out to meet him. I almost run straight into Nat, who's standing there by the stairs as though he were about to go down to get the door. He takes a long look at me, and something in his face changes.

"What are you dressed like that for?"

"I have a date with Astor," I say. "I'm going to Astor's place out in the canyons."

Nat's eyes narrow slightly. "Don't you have anything less revealing to wear? Come on."

He takes hold of my arm, pulling me back towards my room. How dare he do that? He's been more or less ignoring me for days, yet now he thinks he can do that?

"Let go of me, Nat."

"Summer, you're *not* going to a guy's house alone dressed like that. You know what that could lead to."

"Since when do you care?" I demand.

Nat looks hurt by that. "I've always cared, Summer. More than you think. And I don't want you making a big mistake. You shouldn't even be with this Fairway guy."

"You can't tell me who to see and who not to see," I argue. "I'm not your little sister. In fact, forget that, because Rachel wouldn't let you treat her like this either. I can make my own decisions. I'm not a little girl anymore, Nat, whatever you might think."

"I know that," Nat says, running his hand through his hair. "Believe me, I'm all too aware of it. And you're right, you can do what you want, but it doesn't stop me from caring. Too much, maybe."

What does he mean by that? Does he really mean… no, I can't think like that, because I'm about to go out with Astor, and I can't have the thought of that making my heart pound in my chest while I'm with him. I have to ask, though. "What are you saying, Nat?"

Nat shakes his head. "I can't go there."

"Why not?" I demand. "Why can't you just say what you feel? Is it so difficult that you have to walk around pretending I don't exist?"

"There are more than my feelings at stake here, Summer. I have a girlfriend. A girlfriend I'm committed to. Then there are other people too. You think that if I suddenly say that I'm attracted to you, that will magically make everything all right?"

"So you do care about me?" I look at him until Nat has to look away.

"Of course I care about you. I always have."

That should feel good. If anything, it makes me angry. "You knew how I felt about you," I say. "You've always known. If you felt the same, why go and get yourself another girl?"

"That's complicated," Nat says.

I shake my head. "It seems pretty simple to me."

"Then you haven't grown up as much as you think," Nat snaps, then stops himself. "I'm sorry, but things *are* difficult. What did you expect me to do, Summer. It was three years, and you were a long way away. I don't do long distance, because it doesn't work. Yes, when I saw your photo it brought back memories, and when I saw you in person every feeling I ever had for you came back, but it can't work. I have a girlfriend, and you… you're meant to be dating a TV star, remember? That's kind of hard to compete with, so nothing can ever happen."

"We could try," I say. "I *want* to try. I've cared for you forever, you know that. Anyone else... even Astor, he's not you. All those years when you just didn't want to know... you don't know how much that hurt, Nat."

He takes me by the shoulders then. "I'm sorry. I never meant for it to be like this, but it's too messed up now. I'm thinking about you constantly. In my dreams, every day. It isn't fair to Chrissy. She wants us to move further on in our relationship, and I'm not even thinking about her. I can't do this, Summer, and I don't think you can either."

I nod, moving back from him and going to the bathroom I share with Rachel to check on my makeup. There's a smear around my eye where tears have started to fall. I wipe it away and reapply makeup.

"You're right," I say. "I can't do that. I'm not about to break things up with you and Chrissy, that's up to you if you want to do it, and I'm not even going to consider dating you if you're still with her. Now, that's Astor at the door, so you'll have to excuse me."

Nat reaches out for my arm again, and this time I step past him. "You've just said that we aren't together, Nat, and even if we were, I wouldn't let you just go around grabbing me."

"But you're still going out?" Nat asks. "After all this, you're still going with him, even though you know it will hurt me?"

I shrug. "You've hurt me for years, Nat, and at least I gave you a chance to be happy with me. It's you who hooked up with Chrissy. If you can't act on what you feel for me, then why should I be unhappy? Astor is amazing. He's a wonderful, sweet, gentle guy who also happens to be incredibly hot."

"Now you're pushing him in my face," Nat says.

I shake my head. "No. I'm telling you that my happiness isn't up to you, Nat. If you'd wanted to be with me, that would have been great. If you can't give up Chrissy… well, she's a lucky girl, and maybe you should try thinking about her instead of me. If you can't, I'm still not going to drop everything while you figure out what you want. I'm going to go after what I want."

"And that's Astor?" Nat asks.

I shrug. "He makes me happy, and that's more than what you're doing right now, Nat. Now, I'm going downstairs, because he's been waiting at the door far too long. And I'm doing it in this dress. If you can't cope with that, then that's your problem, not mine."

I walk away from him then, heading downstairs to the door. Astor's waiting there, looking amazing in a casual shirt and jeans. Maybe I've overdressed for the occasion. Or maybe not, given the way he looks when he sees me.

"You look amazing," he says, almost as soon as he sees me.

"Sorry it took me so long to answer the door," I say.

"It's a woman's prerogative to take her time about getting ready for a date," Astor replies, with another glance at me. "Especially when she ends up looking like that."

He kisses me then. I think about Nat, and wonder if he's watching. Then I smile to myself, decide that I don't care, and kiss Astor back.

Chapter 9

Astor drives me up into the canyons, around the twists and turns of the climbing roads that give me a great view of the scenery around us. There are small streams down below, along with trees everywhere the rocky hillsides aren't rising up above road level.

"This is a beautiful place to live," I say.

"I guess," he replies. "Your aunt's place is pretty cool too, though, and this can feel a little out of the way sometimes."

Maybe, but I can also see how Astor might need somewhere out of the way, occasionally. His house sits off a small side road, with great views out over one of the canyons. It's a big, modern place that looks like it must have cost a fortune. But then, Astor can afford it. That's kind of strange, the idea of a guy my age having a place like this.

"This is all yours?" I ask.

Astor smiles. "It isn't like I have to share it."

"I guess what I mean is where are your parents?"

Astor shakes his head. "I wanted my own place, so I bought one. They have a pretty good place of their own, back in Malibu, but I wanted somewhere I could just be *me,* you know?"

I think I understand, but it isn't easy. I know that I'm going to go to college, move out, get a place of my own, but until then, I like the idea of having my family around me. Even if it's only Aunt Sookie at the moment. Besides, with Rachel, Drew and Nat at the beach house, I never really have time to feel alone.

"So," I say, "do I get the grand tour?"

Astor nods. "I'd like that."

He shows me inside, into an entrance hall that reaches right up to a skylight in the roof. Off that, there's a kitchen where everything is finished in white tiles that reflect a lot of the light coming in through large windows onto a breakfast bar running across it. There's also a lounge, which I can kind of tell belongs to a boy living alone. It's neat, in a way that says Astor has cleaners who come in every day, but everything about it is set up for him more than for a family. There's a large white leather armchair in the middle of the floor, in front of an even bigger TV with a collection of games consoles hooked up to it. There's a couch running most of the length of one wall, and another is taken up with row after row of games, DVDs, books and magazines. There's even a dried sea star hanging on the wall as an ornament.

There's another room opposite it that's more of a study. It has a desk with an expensive looking computer on it, a phone, a few pages of what look like scripts and not much else. I can imagine Astor in here looking over potential roles, or talking to his agent, or something like that. There's a pool out back, with a great view out over the surrounding canyons and a garden that's as neatly maintained as the rest of the place. I guess Astor can afford gardeners too. Astor doesn't show me upstairs yet, heading back to the kitchen instead.

"You must be hungry," he says, moving over to the kitchen's oven.

"You cooked for me?" Just the thought of Astor working away in the kitchen comes as a shock, but he shakes his head.

"My housekeeper Rosa made something and left it in the oven," Astor says. "Actually, I should check on it."

He takes out two plates piled high with chicken and fresh vegetables. It's hard to think of the kind of life Astor must have. Thanks to the money he's earned from TV, he can have anything he wants. He can have people who can clean his house and leave food waiting for him and his date. He can have a house that looks like everything is custom designed for him. I have to admit, it's all pretty impressive, even though there's part of me that can see why he's enjoyed spending time down in the beach house so much. It isn't just that I'm there, though I'd like to think that's a big part of it. It's the fact that it's something so... normal.

"Did I tell you how great that dress looks on you?" Astor says as we start to eat.

I smile. "A few times."

Astor smiles back. "Well, you deserve all the compliments I can give you."

We eat slowly, talking about what it's like for Astor working in TV, our time at the acting academy, and Aunt Sookie's place.

"It must be good having so many friends around you," Astor says.

I think of Nat, and Drew; of how it isn't always that easy, but I nod as I think about Rachel and what a good friend she is. "It is pretty good. But you must have *some* friends. I know you say they're all part of your job, but that doesn't stop them from being friends, does it?"

Astor shrugs. "I hang out with some of the others on the cast of my shows, but there's always that feeling of 'what if the show's cancelled next week?' Would they still want to know me then?"

I move closer to kiss him. "The good news is that I'll want to know you no matter what. Show or no show."

"I know," Astor says. "You aren't like most girls, Summer."

"Let me guess," I say, "they just want to say that they've been with a TV star?"

Astor nods. "That, or they want to *be* TV stars. And if they're more normal, I don't have enough in common with them to make things work. You're different. You kind of know what it's like, because of your aunt's school, but you're normal too. Well, not just normal. You're pretty, and smart, and…"

"You're pretty wonderful yourself," I point out.

We finish dinner and head through into the lounge, where it turns out that Astor has plenty of old movies in his collection. I guess, spending so much time with Aunt Sookie, I've always loved that kind of thing, and Astor seems to know it, because the next few hours turn into a movie marathon.

We start out sitting on that long couch for it, because that's the only spot with room for us both. Not to mention the popcorn Astor produces a couple of minutes in. We sit close enough that I can feel every breath he takes, and hear him whispering some of the movie lines the instant before they come out of the speakers.

"You really do love these, don't you?" I ask.

Astor nods. "It's kind of why I'm taking so many acting lessons."

"So it's not just an excuse to hang around me at the school?"

Astor kisses me. "That too, but I could do that at the beach. I'm taking the lessons because I want to get better at this. I see all those old stars and I think... well, what if I get my parts just because I'm young and good-looking, not because I can actually act like that? What if I don't get roles like that when I'm older, because no one thinks I can do it?"

I cup his jaw in my hand. There's something almost vulnerable about Astor in that moment that I doubt he's let anyone else see. I kiss him softly. "I doubt that will happen."

I get up to fetch a drink from the kitchen, and I see how dark it has gotten. I've obviously been there longer than I thought. Astor follows me through to the kitchen, and obviously sees me checking my watch.

"I'm not boring you that much, am I?"

"You're not boring me at all," I say. "I'm just worried that I should be getting back. It's later than I thought."

"So why not stay over?" Astor says, and then holds up a hand to cut me off before I can reply. "I mean that I have a couple of spare bedrooms, and it seems like a shame to cut off the movie marathon here. I can take you home in the morning. If you want to phone home and tell them what you're doing…"

I know I probably shouldn't, but there's something so good about the evening that I don't want it to end. So I phone Rachel, telling her what I'm doing. She seems pretty relaxed about it, and maybe a little excited.

"Actually," she says, "that could work pretty well. Sure, I'll tell everyone where you are."

"Just be sure to tell them that Astor and I are in separate rooms."

"Will you be, though? I mean, I would *definitely* go there with Astor Fairway."

"*Rachel.*"

Rachel hangs up, and I head back into the lounge with Astor, where we settle into his chair again, so that I'm almost sitting in his lap as we watch the movie that's in front of us. Not that we watch much of it. Pretty soon, we're just making out, kissing so deeply that everything on the screen seems to fade into the background. Astor's hands are on my hair, moving down across my shoulders, moving over my back…

I look up, and my eyes happen to see the sea star on the wall. I find myself thinking back. I would have been… what? Eight? That's right. I was eight, Nat was nine, and Aunt Sookie had taken all of us to Sea World in San Diego. There were sea stars in a tank, and I was watching them, reaching in after them for one of the biggest ones, wanting to know what it felt like.

I remember a bigger kid snatching it from my hands as I pulled it out of the water. "Little kids shouldn't have sea stars," he said.

"Give it back!"

"Make me."

I remember him doubling up then, and Nat stepping past him, ready to hit him again. I remember him picking up the sea star and putting it in my hands.

My mind snaps back to the present, where Astor's hands are sliding under the straps of my dress. My hands go to his.

"Astor, no."

"No?" Astor freezes, and I practically jump off him.

"I… I can't."

"Why not?" He sounds genuinely puzzled.

What can I say? Because we got to that point and I started thinking about Nat? "It's just too much, too fast," I say. "When I said I'd stay over, I didn't know that this was what you had in mind. I'm sorry if I wasn't clear. I… if you want me to go home now, that's fine."

Astor shakes his head, reaching out for me and placing a gentle kiss on my forehead. *"I'm* sorry," he says. "I got carried away. And you don't have to go home. I'll drive you back in the morning. I meant it before, when I said that I have plenty of guest rooms here. And I meant it about finishing the movie marathon too, if you want."

I nod. This time though, we both sit on the couch, and I spend as much time staring at that sea star as I do at the movie. Staring at it, and glancing at Astor. He looks like he's trying to enjoy the movie now, so I try too. Somehow, it just isn't the same.

Chapter 10

Astor drives me back early the next morning. Early enough that I can still make my run with Drew along the beach, grabbing some running clothes out of the laundry basket and getting changed downstairs so that I don't wake Rachel. I figure that just because I had a great night, that doesn't give me the right to crash into the room we share.

Drew is waiting for me on the beach by the time I'm ready, though he seems kind of serious this morning. Quieter. He has another flower for me, this one apparently from a different patch of them the other way along the beach.

"I'll race you to it," he says, and sprints off without waiting for a reply.

"Hey! No fair!"

I race after him up the beach, finally catching him when we're almost far enough out to turn back. We take the jog back slower, but Drew is still kind of playful with it, speeding up and slowing down so that I have to work to keep pace with him. Finally, I set off ahead of him, making him keep pace with me instead.

Him making breakfast has gotten to be a ritual once we get back from our run, and even though I had some cereal at Astor's place, I'm still hungry after that run. This morning though, I decide to help out in the kitchen, frying ham and eggs while Drew takes care of the rest. There's something so sweet about him when he's like this, though I guess that sweet is one word he won't want to hear used about himself.

"Why aren't you like this more often?" I ask. "I mean, I remember the way you used to be, but now you seem to spend so much time hunting after girls, playing the football hero…"

Drew shrugs. "What can I say? I have an image to keep up. You think anyone back in San Francisco will want to know me if I'm not what they expect me to be?"

"You aren't there now," I point out. "And anyway, why do you care?"

"Everyone cares what people think, Summer. As for why I'm different here… maybe you just bring out a different side of me."

"Just me?" After everything last night, I'm not sure I want to have this conversation now.

Drew shakes his head though. "Part of it is being back here too. There are so many good memories here, I guess it's easier to be who I used to be. Now, are you going to wake Aunt Sookie? She'll need to be at the acting academy soon."

"I'll wake everyone up," I say, because it's starting to get a little later. "I figure that if I've been up all this time, they can be too."

I wake Aunt Sookie first, along with Rachel. Aunt Sookie hurries to get ready for work, barely taking anything to eat for breakfast. She hugs me, and even after just waking up, she seems a little tired.

"I'll see you down at my school later, Summer," she says, hurrying out while Rachel grabs the shower. While she's doing that, to my surprise and I think Drew's shock, Ryan pads out of the bedroom Rachel and I share. He pauses just long enough to grab some of the ham, but he looks pretty sheepish in the face of Drew's stare.

"Hey, Summer," he says. "Hey, Drew."

Drew's look isn't particularly friendly, and Ryan turns to me.

"I guess I'd better... well, would you tell Rachel I'll see her later?"

"Sure," I say, trying to keep things casual, even though Drew obviously doesn't want to. "Goodbye, Ryan."

Ryan nods and leaves, a little before Rachel finally comes out of the shower, drying her hair with a towel.

"Did Ryan go already?"

Drew looks at her, and he looks almost disgusted. "You didn't. With *him*?"

"What's wrong with Ryan? At least I care about him, which is more than you can say about most of the girls you sleep with."

"But that… that's *different*."

"And that," Rachel shoots back, "is a *total* double standard. Isn't it, Summer? I mean, you stayed the night at Astor's place…"

"Nothing happened," I say, not telling her about the moment when it almost did. Definitely not wanting to say it in front of Drew. It occurs to me that I've somehow managed to plant myself firmly in the middle of a brewing sibling argument. Both Rachel and Drew are staring at one another in an angry silence.

"I'm just going to go check on Nat," I say, because it seems like the quickest way to get away from them. "He should be awake by now. I mean, I knocked loud enough."

"Loud enough to wake Ryan, at least," Drew says.

Rachel shoots him a nasty look. "Oh, would you just grow up?"

I get out of there pretty quickly, heading for Nat and Drew's room. I knock, waiting for Nat to answer. When he doesn't, I finally push open the door and realize that he isn't in the room. He's obviously gone out while I was with Drew. I head back to the kitchen table, eating quickly while Rachel and Drew continue the icy stare-down that has developed between them. It's enough to make me give up on breakfast early.

"I'm just going to go look for Nat," I say.

"Sure," Rachel says, not taking her eyes off Drew.

Drew shrugs. "Fine."

I practically run out of there, making it out onto the beach before the shouting begins. I know I should probably try to stop Drew and Rachel from fighting, but I know from experience that there's no point trying to get between them until they're done. They don't fight often, but when they do, it's a good idea to be somewhere else.

I settle for heading down the beach the way Drew and I didn't run earlier, figuring that if Nat is anywhere, he's going to be there. I finally spot him sitting on an outcrop of rocks, where he's writing in a small, pocket sized journal bound in leather. He puts it away in the pocket of the deep cream shirt he's wearing as I get closer, standing and brushing off his jeans as he steps back down onto the sand.

"Hey, Nat," I say. "What are you doing all the way out here? We missed you at breakfast. I did, anyway. Rachel and Drew are just gearing up for open warfare."

I smile as I say it, but Nat doesn't return it.

"I wasn't hungry," he says, moving closer and sitting down on the sand. As I sit down beside him, those deep green eyes of his seem to burn into mine. "How was your date? I know you didn't come back last night."

"My date was good," I say.

"Just good?" Nat asks, and there's a sharp note in it. I guess he's made the same assumption that Rachel did. It annoys me a little.

"Nothing happened, but who *wouldn't* want to be with Astor Fairway. I mean, he's everything a girl could want, all wrapped up in one boyfriend, right? He's smart, he's funny, he's successful, rich, good-looking…"

I don't know why I'm doing it. Maybe because I want some kind of reaction from Nat. If that's what I want, I certainly get one.

"He sounds perfect," Nat says. "I guess it depends on whether you want perfect. I hear some girls prefer their boyfriends a little more flawed and troubled."

"And that's you?" I ask. I shake my head. Nat isn't flawed, or troubled. At least, I don't think he is.

Nat's gaze is intense. It's like he can see right through me. "It is today, and I guess it isn't going to get much better."

"Why?" I ask. This isn't like Nat. It isn't like him at all.

"I called Chrissy last night, after you left for Astor's place. I know I shouldn't want you, but I do, and I can't ignore that."

I swallow, thinking that I know what might be coming. "What are you saying, Nat?"

"I broke up with Chrissy last night. I told her that it wasn't fair to keep seeing her, to keep moving forward with her, when there was someone else I couldn't stop thinking about." He reaches out for me. "You, Summer. I can't stop thinking about you."

He kisses me there on the beach, his lips pressing into mine the way I've wanted them to for so long. So many years waiting for this, and now it has finally arrived, the kiss is amazing. Nat's a great kisser, taking control of it and kissing me powerfully, searchingly. He kisses me until I can barely think straight, but right now it feels like I'm having plenty of problems with that anyway.

It's like the previous night with Astor. I'm kissing Nat, but I'm not thinking about him. Not all the time, at least. For some of it, I'm swept up in the sheer physical closeness of him, but I also find myself thinking about Drew, and the side of himself he's shown me in the last few days. I think about how he looked getting out of the pool, and how much he obviously wants me, too.

Then there's Astor. I told Nat at the start, he's pretty much the perfect guy. *And* he's the guy I dated just last night. The guy I thought I might… the guy I came so close to taking it further with. Yet I didn't, thanks to all my thoughts of Nat, and now here Nat is, kissing me. Yet I don't know what I want to do. I just don't know.

I push back from Nat, standing, and he looks like I've just slapped him. "What's wrong," he asks. "I thought this was what you wanted."

"I wanted you to be sure about what you want," I say, "but now that you are, that doesn't suddenly mean I am, Nat."

"You don't feel the way I do?" Nat asks. "You had me break up with Chrissy for nothing?"

I shake my head. "*You* broke up with her, Nat. I didn't tell you to. I didn't even know about it until you told me."

"And now you don't want me."

That makes me step back. "I didn't say *that* either. Of course I want you. There's a part of me that wants you more than anything, but it isn't the only part of me, Nat. I can't just turn off what I feel for other people just because it suits you."

Nat follows. "So now I'm the one left hanging while *you* decide what you want?"

"I don't know what I want!" I practically yell at him, knowing that I have to get out of there. I can't keep having this conversation. Not when it will inevitably bring in Drew at some point. Not when I don't know the answer to the questions he's asking. So I turn and hurry off down the beach, back towards the house.

Rachel and Drew are doing the quiet staring thing again when I get in, but right then, that just makes it easier for me to want to get out of there. I head past them, walking quickly up to the room I share with Rachel to grab my purse and my car keys. Then I head out front, knowing that there's only one place I'm going to be able to think.

I start driving towards Aunt Sookie's school. I see Nat in the rearview mirror, but I ignore him. He's looking so anguished and a part of me wants to stop the car to rush out and hold him, to kiss him, but I don't. I've loved him for so long, and he has ignored me for so long. I would go to him in a heartbeat, but now, now that I have opened my eyes to my feelings for Drew and even Astor, things have become more complicated than I've ever imagined. Aunt Sookie was right. This summer is going to be really different, a summer everyone will remember.

Chapter 11

By the time I get to Aunt Sookie's acting academy, I know what I'm doing there. I'm going to tell her everything that has been happening and get her advice, even if it means answering some awkward questions when it comes to Drew, Astor and Nat. I pull up and head inside, going straight to the classroom in the old theater where I know Sookie will be teaching one of her more advanced classes.

"The trick is to not be too large, when it comes to TV. The cameras are right in your face, so you have to be much more subtle than on a stage."

That isn't Aunt Sookie's voice. Instead, when I step into the old theater space, it's Astor up on the stage, leading the class. My aunt is nowhere to be seen. For now though, I'm too caught up in watching Astor teach. It's kind of strange seeing a kid my age telling adults how to act in front of the camera, but I guess he knows as much about it as anyone. He's confident and cool, as if he has been teaching for years. I take a seat and start to watch.

He tells a story about his time on set as a kid, all about the kind of things that happened with the show.

"Most of the time, when I was just a little kid, I couldn't remember a whole script, so they had me improvise, and then the other actors would try to keep things on track. Well, that worked pretty well, because it was spontaneous. That's the hardest part of acting. Making it look like things are happening to you for the first time, when in fact, you've read the whole script and you know exactly what's going to happen next."

Astor has them working different acting exercises next. In one, he has them act the same short lines out four or five times in a row, to force everyone there to try to find ways to keep their delivery fresh. There's something so straightforward and down to earth about him when he's here, and all the students seem to appreciate the instruction they're getting.

Eventually though, the class ends, and Astor walks over to me. He brushes his fingers along my arm, and just that touch is enough to send my nerves tingling. His hands drift up to my head, holding me as though he might kiss me any minute.

"I know we only saw each other this morning," he says with a smile, "but I'm glad you're here now too."

He does kiss me then, softly and fleetingly. "I'm sorry I moved too fast last night," Astor says. "I couldn't help myself. I don't think I've ever met anyone quite like you, Summer, and I just wanted... well, I guess I wanted to show you that.

"You make me so happy, Summer," he says. "I don't care if we just talk, hang out, or what, I love being with you. Come on."

He takes my hand, taking me out of the theater before I can find Aunt Sookie, then down to the beach, where we find a small restaurant with views out over the ocean. It's the kind of place most people would have to book weeks in advance to get a table in, but Astor just walks right in. Apparently, they know him.

"The manager's daughters and wife are big fans of my show," he whispers to me by way of an explanation. It also explains why he seems to know the menu by heart, ordering the seafood salad without even looking at it. I do the same. It's delicious, but when, halfway through it, Astor pulls out a small box, my heart leaps into my mouth just the same.

It isn't a large box. It's a light baby blue with a white bow, and it sits neatly on the table between us when Astor puts it down.

"Would you accept this from me?" Astor asks. "I was passing a store on the way to the academy, and I saw it, and it was just perfect for you."

I start to shake my head. "Astor, I couldn't accept anything expensive like this. That wouldn't be…"

"Relax," Astor says with a smile. "Remember that I have the money. If I want to spend it on you, please just go with that. Besides, this is just something small."

He holds the box out to me and I take it, unfastening the bow. When I open it, I gasp, because the pendant within is beautiful. It's small, and silver, and it's in the shape of a sea shell. It's perfect. Astor has found exactly the kind of thing I might actually wear, and he helps me to put it on now, fastening it around my neck, before returning to his seat and reaching out to hold my hand.

"Maybe that will do something to remind all the guys who must be itching for a shot with you that we're together," Astor says. I find myself thinking of Nat and Drew again, but right then the moment is too perfect to think too hard.

"This is amazing," I say. "How did you guess that it would be right for me?"

Astor smiles, shaking his head. "It doesn't take a lifetime to know who someone you care about is. As soon as I saw you, Summer, I felt like I'd known you all my life."

"That's…" I don't know what to say to that. It's romantic, and it also feels true. Like I've known Astor forever too, rather than just a few weeks.

"Listen, Summer," Astor looks a little worried suddenly. "The necklace is to show you that I'm serious about us, even though I'm going to have to go away for a while soon."

"You're leaving?" I can hardly believe that. We've only just started dating.

"It's part of why I'm doing the extra work with your aunt," Astor says. "There are some movie roles I'm up for, and I start work on one in North Carolina next week."

North Carolina? That's a long way. Will it work, us being so far apart so soon? It seems, though, that isn't what Astor has in mind.

"I want you to come with me," he says. "For the first week or so at least. I mean, you're still on summer break, so it isn't like you're going to miss school, and from all the work you've done at the acting academy, I guess you'd like hanging out on set, and... well, I'd like you there. A lot. So what do you say?"

I want to say yes, but I know I can't, and Astor seems to sense it, because he moves away from me slightly.

"Well," he says, "I guess I have your number if you don't want to do it."

"I want to," I say. "I really want to, but I have to be here to help Aunt Sookie. I can't just drop everything."

"I understand," Astor says, and he leans across the table to kiss me. "I'm just worried. I want to keep seeing you. I want you to be my girl, but that won't be easy if we're all that way apart. You won't be there with me."

I shake my head. "It isn't like you'll be lonely. There will be people all around you on set."

"They won't be *you*," Astor says urgently, frowning. He reaches out to take my hand. "At least tell me you'll think about visiting me up in North Carolina. I know you need to be here, what with Sookie being sick and everything, but maybe there will be time?"

"What?" I say.

"You're right," Astor says, frowning again. He shakes his head and stands up. "Forget I said anything, Summer. Of course you're going to want to stay here to look after your aunt while she's ill. I shouldn't have asked."

"It's not that," I say, wondering if I look as puzzled as I feel. "What I mean is, what do you mean, Aunt Sookie's sick?"

"You don't know?" Astor sits back down, looking at me intently. "Sorry, I just assumed that she would have told you. I mean, I found out because we've been spending so much time together for the lessons, and she had to go to the doctor..."

"What's wrong with her?" I ask, wondering if Astor has it wrong. Aunt Sookie can't be sick, can she? She would have said something. Except I remember how tired she has been, and how careful she's been about what she eats. *Something* hasn't been right.

Astor looks uncomfortable. "Um... I guess that if she hasn't said something, then I probably shouldn't either. I mean, it's for her to tell you, not me, and I'd hate to be the one who broke her confidence."

"What's wrong with her, Astor?" I demand, not caring about any of that. "If something's wrong with her, I have a right to know. If you care about me, you'll tell me, rather than keeping secrets from me."

"Diabetes," Astor says simply. "I'm not sure which type, only that it's pretty advanced, genetics or something plus her diet for the last decade. She was talking about not just having to take medication, have shots, but she mentioned having had surgery a couple of months ago."

"What kind of surgery?" I ask.

"I don't know," Astor insists. "Honestly, Summer, I'd tell you if I did."

It doesn't seem fair. It doesn't seem fair that Aunt Sookie should have something like this happen to her. She's done so much to care for others, whether it's inviting inner city kids into her school to keep them out of trouble and away from gangs, or taking me and the others in every summer, or just doing so much to help her students with their dreams.

Diabetes explains so much about what has been happening with her, but I realize I don't know anywhere near as much as I should about the disease. I didn't even know that there was surgery for it. I thought it was just a case of staying on insulin and trying to adjust your life.

Why didn't Aunt Sookie tell me any of this? I know the answer to that. I have the memories of her caring for me, kissing my knee whenever I fell down, helping me deal with anything that hurt or ached. She's trying to protect me from this.

She can't protect me from how much this moment hurts though. She can't protect me from thinking back to all the moments I've had with her, whether it's helping at her school, or watching while she taught Drew and Nat to throw a football, or letting Rachel play with her professional actor's makeup kit. If anything, not telling me just makes it worse, because I don't know how I'm going to talk to her about this.

Astor comes and puts his arms around me, and I realize that I'm crying.

"Don't you..." I think back to all the other days with Astor. "Don't you have rehearsals?"

"They can wait," Astor assures me, holding me tightly. "This is going to be all right Summer. You'll see."

I want to believe him, but right then, it's hard. Something like this… a few minutes ago, I was thinking about whether I could make it to North Carolina, but now I'm wondering how I'll ask Aunt Sookie about what's going on. About how I'll talk to the others about it. Somehow, next to that, everything else seems pretty trivial.

Chapter 12

Astor takes me back to Aunt Sookie's school, only leaving when I assure him that I'm okay. I head inside, looking for my aunt, I find her in her office, which is a converted dressing room behind the main theater space. She's on the phone when I go in, so I start tidying the office. I need to do something. I can't just sit there and wait, because I think I might explode if I did.

The office isn't large, with just enough room for a desk, a computer, a few boxes and some bookshelves, but there's certainly plenty of stuff in here. There are pieces of old costumes and boxes of makeup, old scripts in piles and folders full of administrative details. The result is that it's a space where probably only Aunt Sookie knows where anything is, and where it's a constant battle to keep things neat.

Aunt Sookie smiles at me as I walk in, but keeps talking on the phone. "We were always the most sensitive ones in school," she says. "Nadine, are you sure you don't want me to come up to San Fran? No? Then you should make a trip to the Pad. The kids are enjoying themselves. Rachel seems to have a boyfriend, and Drew is getting along great with Summer. She's helping me out with classes at the school."

Aunt Sookie pauses, listening. "Nat? Oh, he's mostly preoccupied with old friends. Join us for July 4th at least. We'll have barbeques, hot dogs, and everything. You don't have to be there to supervise your husband's company party. It will do fine without you, and you should have some fun. You don't have to keep playing the perfect corporate wife anymore, Nadine. You know it isn't you."

Aunt Sookie starts listening again, and I feel like I'm intruding on a private moment just by being here.

"Yes, I know you used to be good at it, but you're so much more than just arm candy for him. Especially given what happened. And if he's going to spend years cheating on you with his secretary, then he shouldn't make Nat keep that secret. I'm glad Nat finally told you."

I start to wonder if I should leave anyway, but Aunt Sookie just keeps going. Either she doesn't mind me hearing this, or she's angry enough now that she doesn't care.

"No, Nat's fine. I know he was always your baby. I can't believe how much he and Drew have grown. Summer?" Aunt Sookie looks at me. "No, she's dating one of my students. You should see her. Maybe you can when you come down. I'm a very proud aunt these days. Now listen, seriously, come down to my place. We'll do the whole girl thing; maybe go down to Vegas while the kids play at the beach. I know. Listen, anything you want to talk about, I'm there for you. You know that, right? Love you."

Aunt Sookie finally hangs up. I don't know why she let me hear all that. Maybe it was just easier than telling me to go. Maybe she wanted me to know about it. Now that I do… I don't know what to think. It must have been so hard for Nat, if what I've just heard is true. Having to keep a secret like that from his own mother. Having to tell her.

Then again, I guess Aunt Sookie knows a thing or two about keeping secrets right now. After all, there's at least one big thing she didn't tell me about. Maybe that's why she let me hear that. Maybe she's tired of keeping secrets.

"Hey," she says, "what are you doing over here when you could be out enjoying yourself?"

"I wanted to talk," I say.

"About what you just heard?" Sookie shrugs. "Nadine is having a hard time of things, what with the divorce. That's kind of why I asked all the kids down here again. I thought you should know." She looks at me for a few seconds. "That pendant is new, isn't it? Did you just buy it?"

"Astor gave it to me."

She nods. "I'd guessed that he was serious about you when he invited you to stay over. Well, he's a good boy, but obviously, you want to be careful, Summer. Don't go rushing too far, too soon."

Most times, I might have talked that through with her, but right now, it isn't what I want us to talk about. "Astor told me something."

"What did he tell you?" my aunt asks. "That he has to go away for a while? It's only a job, Summer. He'll be back if he really cares about you."

I shake my head. "It isn't that. It's something... well, he kind of told me accidentally. You shouldn't blame him for it, I mean, because I think he really respects you."

"Well, *that* sounds kind of ominous," Aunt Sookie says with another smile.

I force myself to say it. "He said that you were sick. Diabetes."

Her smile freezes and then disappears. "I guess I shouldn't have thought I could keep it a secret."

"So it's true?" I ask, moving to sit across from her. "Astor didn't make a mistake?"

Aunt Sookie shakes her head. "He didn't make a mistake. I have a rare form of diabetes. I've probably had it for a while...a combination of genetics and my lifestyle.

You see, after my divorce, which hit me hard, I had let myself go with eating badly, gaining weight, not sleeping, not exercising and not taking care of myself for years. I mean I wasn't very heavy, but for my body type I was, and that combined with genetics helped contribute to what I have." Aunt Sookie smiled. "Thank God for you kids. You guys helped get me out of bed in the mornings. I looked forward to having all of you every summer because of all the fun we would have. Nadine and your mom thought it would be the thing to snap me out of the state I was in. You know…it worked! But I already had some of the conditions, and haven't treated it. I'm sorry I didn't tell you before, Summer. I'm trying to get better, and with treatment, I'll be fine."

"But that's…"

She reaches across the table to put a hand over mine. "This is why I didn't tell you. You don't need to get upset, Summer. I don't want to ruin your summer. I don't want to ruin the Donovan kids' summer. Nat, Drew and Rachel are already going through enough with Nadine and their father. Hearing about him cheating on their mom must be like him cheating on them. It's hard enough for them without adding this to it."

"But they'll want to know," I insist, looking around the office. Looking anywhere but at my aunt, because I think if I keep looking at her I'll start crying.

"They might," Aunt Sookie admits. "But look at how upset you are right now, Summer. I never wanted to hurt you like that. I don't want to hurt them like that either."

I shake my head. "What hurts is that you didn't trust me enough to tell me what was going on with you. Did you think that I wouldn't want to help?" I stare at her. "Did you think that you were just going to do this whole thing alone? I mean, you're sick, and I... I've just been enjoying myself when I could have been helping you."

Aunt Sookie moves around her desk then, perching on it and putting a hand on my shoulder. "I *want* you to enjoy yourself, Summer. I'm not going to let some stupid illness take over your life when I don't even want it to take over mine. Okay, so there are some tough moments, but I'm trying not to worry too much."

"Trying not to worry?" I shake my head, hardly able to believe it. "You're seriously ill. How can you not worry?"

Aunt Sookie hugs me then, holding me close for several seconds. "I'm not worrying because there's no *point* in worrying. I'm going to do everything I need to in order to get better, and although diabetes is potentially very serious, it isn't impossible to cope with. I've already had a round of surgery for this, so it's mostly a question of recovering and seeing how it goes."

"Surgery?" I look at her in surprise. Aunt Sookie has had surgery and she didn't tell anyone?

"Sometimes, with some forms of diabetes, surgery can help," she says. "In theory, it might even cure me. If it doesn't, then it's just a case of making sure I stay on the right drugs to manage it, and either way it goes, I'm going to have to make a few changes to my lifestyle and diet."

"Which explains all the health food in the fridge," I say. "And why you haven't been eating the things Nat and Drew have put together."

Aunt Sookie smiles then. "Well, it isn't exactly the healthiest food, is it?"

I can't help smiling back at her.

"This isn't the end of the world, Summer. It isn't even the end of me having a good time. I'll just be more thirsty and tired physically, but it's just something I have to deal with."

I nod. "You have to take care of yourself, though," I say. "Take things slowly. Do whatever the doctors say. I can help with the school. I guess Drew, Nat and Rachel can help too. I know you want to treat everything like it's normal, but you can't keep putting in the hours you have been if it's just going to exhaust you. You have to give yourself the time to recover."

"I'm trying to take things a little easier," Aunt Sookie admits.

A thought comes to me. "What about Mom? Does she know about this?"

Aunt Sookie shakes her head. "No. I didn't tell her. I don't want to worry her either."

"But she's your sister," I say. "She deserves to know."

"And I'll tell her, in my own time." Aunt Sookie's expression is serious and she pulls back, going back to her seat behind the desk. "Summer, this is going to be fine, you know. Pretty soon, we'll all be wondering what the fuss was about while I go skydiving with you, or surfing with the boys, or on a trip to Paris with Nadine and your mom, or something."

I hope that she's right. I know that diabetes isn't as serious as some illnesses, but I also know that it can still do serious damage. It can even be fatal. I'm worried that my aunt is so busy trying to pretend that everything is fine that she might not do everything she needs to do in order to get better.

"I'm serious about helping out more at the school though," I say. "I can handle a lot of the classes here. The ones that aren't too advanced, at least. Even some of those, maybe."

"I don't doubt you could do the advanced ones if you wanted," Aunt Sookie says, "but remember that a lot of the time, those students are paying for my teaching. I'll keep going with those, and the rest until I decide otherwise. Summer, I'm not just going to sit at home all day."

I know I'm not going to be able to argue with her on this, so I nod. "Okay, but please, *ask* if you want help. You shouldn't have to do something like this alone."

"Oh, darling, I'm not alone." Aunt Sookie smiles as she looks over at me. "I have a wonderful trio of young people back in my house, all of whom are like family to me. I have you here, and you're more like a daughter to me than a niece. Who cares if I'm sick? I have everything I could ever want right now."

Chapter 13

I go running with Drew as usual the next morning, but it doesn't feel like there's anything usual about it. I was expecting Aunt Sookie to just announce her illness to the others the moment she got home last night, but she didn't. Maybe it was because we got back pretty late, and Rachel was out with Ryan for a lot of the evening, so it never seemed like there was a good time, but it means that I have the knowledge of Aunt Sookie being sick bubbling up inside me. I need to tell someone about it.

For now though, I just run with Drew, starting out on the route we normally take but then heading down towards the spur of rock where I found Nat writing the other day. I'm not sure why I go that way. Maybe I just want to do something different, or maybe it feels like a good place to talk things over. Either way, I'm concentrating so hard on what I'm going to say by the time we get there that I'm not paying attention to my footing.

I slip on the soft sand, and for a moment, I tumble towards the rocks. When I'm falling towards them, they look a lot more jagged than they did when I was just running. I brace myself, trying to stop myself hitting my head on that brutally hard surface, but I know that it isn't going to work. This is going to hurt.

Strong arms wrap around me, catching me. Drew lifts me up completely, carrying me a little way further up the beach, away from the rocks and the soft sand, turning me as he puts me down, so that we're just inches away from one another. I can feel the adrenaline pumping through me, my heart beating faster even than it was during the run. Drew's the same, his breathing coming quickly for a second or two.

If Drew hadn't been there…

"Thanks for saving me," I say. It doesn't feel like enough somehow.

Drew seems to think it is though, pulling me down gently to sit by him on the sand. "You don't need to thank me. Are you okay?"

I nod.

"I don't just mean with the rocks," he says. "You've been distracted by something since we started running. Is it Sookie, and how ill she is?"

I look at him, my eyes widening slightly. Drew takes my hand in his.

"I pay attention," he says, "and I got the rest out of one of her students. I just want you to know that you can count on me."

"I know I can, Drew," I say, still surprised that he knows. Did everyone know but me? "Actually, I wanted to ask you…"

"If you need me to help out at the school, I can."

That's almost exactly what I was going to ask. I nod. "She's so determined to keep going, but I figure that if we take over some of her classes for the rest of the summer, that will give her the time to recover."

Kailin Gow

Drew puts an arm around me then. "I'd love to do
it, Summer. Sookie's okay with us teaching her classes?"

I nod. "She thinks we can do it."

Drew smiles. "That's good to hear. I mean, it's a
big responsibility."

And from what I've seen of Drew, he doesn't do
responsibility. This is a whole other side of him.

"It's going to be okay with Sookie," Drew
promises, and he's so confident of that it's hard to argue
with it. I love the way his arms around me feel then, so
strong and safe, so that I feel almost tiny pressed against
him. I know I should say something; change the subject
somehow.

"Are you still mad at Rachel for sleeping with
Ryan?" I ask, because it's the only thing I can think of.

Drew shakes his head. "I guess she's right. I was
kind of a hypocrite about that one. I think what made me so
angry... well, part of it is just that I'm pretty protective
when it comes to Rachel. I mean *I* know what guys can be
like."

"Yes," I say, "you do."

Drew ignores that. "I was also pretty worried she was sleeping with him for the wrong reasons. I think she was just lashing out at Mom and Dad getting a divorce, and that's a terrible reason. I know about that, too."

He looks at me and I feel a wave of sympathy for him. I know how hard it must have been for him. Him and Rachel. "For me," he continues, "sleeping with different girls was just a good way to avoid commitment. I mean, if my parents' marriage can fail, how can anything else work? I mean we've been together as a family for all of our lives. Now this? It was pretty bad for all of us." He pauses. "I guess it's even worse for Nat."

"Because he's the one who found out about your father?"

Drew nods. "I don't think I could have handled seeing Dad with his secretary the way Nat did. I don't think I could have handled telling Mom. It should be Dad feeling all the guilt for the divorce, but Nat... I think he feels like it's his fault."

"Oh, poor Nat," I say. "I didn't know you all went through that."

I can see that Drew is trying to be strong and not show any emotion, and I want to comfort him, so I let him hold me. The problem with doing that, of course, is that he's Drew. He only knows one way to interpret that kind of touch. He pulls me in closer to him so that I'm pressed tight against him, his hands drifting over my skin.

"It feels so good to hold you like this, Summer." His lips are so close to mine.

"Drew…"

"I want you to know that since Disneyland, I haven't touched another girl. I haven't *wanted* any girl, except you."

I pull back from him, trying to make a joke of it. "Really? And what happened to the Drew Effect?"

Drew looks torn between his pride and the truth then. "Don't get me wrong, girls still hand me their numbers and come up to me, but I haven't slept with anyone since." He looks at me intensely with his blue eyes. "I don't want to, not anymore."

I put a hand on his arm. "I'm proud of you for that, Drew."

He reaches out, touching the seashell pendant Astor gave me. "Don't be. I should have done it earlier. That way, I wouldn't have you and Rachel seeing me as…"

He doesn't finish it, but he doesn't have to. I look him deep in the eyes. "When I look at you, Drew, I see the kid who cried when he was six because he had scraped his knee. I see the ten year old who used to let me win when we played volleyball. I see the thirteen-year-old who promised to write me every day when we were apart, even though his family moved to San Francisco. I see all of that every time I look at you. I see a wonderful friend I care so much about."

"Friends?" Drew moves in close, kissing me before I can pull away. It's a fast, deep kiss that sends my heart pounding even faster. It's passionate, like white hot fire, but brief, and enough to send a shot of electricity through me, making my toes curl. I blink a couple of times, while he pulls back, holding my shoulders tightly. "Summer, when will you get it? When it comes to you, I can't just be friends. I've tried and tried, but when I look at you, all I want to do is kiss you, to hold you, to make you mine. Mine, Summer. Not Rachel's. Not Nat's, but mine. I always have. Even when we were younger. Even before you were this incredibly beautiful. I loved the you inside and out. You make the world better just by being in it. You make *me* better."

I sit there, stunned. I can't believe he's doing this now. "So why didn't you say anything, then?" I demand. "You've had years, Drew. Why now, when I'm getting serious with Astor?"

"Because seeing you with him has made me realize just how desperate I am to be with you," Drew says. "When I heard you'd gone to his place the other day, I was so terrified about what might happen. I actually thought about going there and bringing you back."

"You didn't!" I shake my head. "You wouldn't."

"I would if that's what it takes to protect you," Drew says simply.

I laugh softly at that, moving back from him slightly. "Drew, I'm not a little girl anymore. I don't need protecting."

I feel someone behind me before I can hear them. When Nat speaks there, I start.

"Do you love him? Is this why you said what you did before?"

Just hearing his voice is enough to send chills down my spine. Drew obviously sees that, because I see his fists clench in anger.

"Do you love him?" Nat repeats as I turn around. He looks so angry standing there. "Do you love that TV star boyfriend of yours?"

I thought he meant Drew. I don't even know why I thought that. Do I love Astor? Part of me wants to say yes there and then, but I don't want to hurt Nat and Drew like that, and there's a part of me that doesn't even see why I should have to give *them* an answer to that question.

"That's between me and Astor, Nat," I say.

"Then maybe you should go tell him," Nat replies, obviously not happy about it. "He came by after you went for your run, and he's waiting in the living room. He says he's leaving for his film shoot." I can see the concern, jealousy and anger there. "Are you going with him, leaving us to go to North Carolina?"

"Aren't you a little late with all this?" Drew demands, standing. "You're with Chrissy."

"Not anymore," Nat snaps back. "I broke it off with her because of the way I feel for Summer."

Drew looks like someone has just thrown cold water on him. He certainly looks like he wants to argue and I... I don't want to be in the middle of it. I want to see Astor before he leaves, so I head back down the beach to the house.

When I get there, Astor is actually pacing back and forth. I didn't even know people did that. He stops as he sees me and rushes over to kiss me.

"I had to see you before I left," he says. "I want you to know that I'm serious about us, Summer. I've never been so certain about anything. Please, come to North Carolina, even if it's just for a day or two. I don't think I can stand not seeing you for weeks on end. Even if you just fly out for the weekends."

"Astor, I…"

He presses an envelope into my hand. "You don't have to arrange anything," he says. "These are the tickets for the flights, so all you have to do is show up. Please say that you will."

I want to, but with Aunt Sookie sick, and everything else that's going on, can I? The answer to that is simple. How can I *not*, when Astor is standing there looking so sad at the thought of being without me?

"Okay," I say. "I'll do it."

He kisses me again then, and this time it's like it goes on forever. He kisses me until we're both deeply out of breath, like he's determined to make as much of a last impression on me as he can before he goes.

"Summer, you just made me the happiest guy in the world." His fingers drift down to the pendant he gave me. "Someday Summer, I'm going to replace that silver seashell pendant for something else more permanent, and I don't want you arguing about it. Clear?"

That makes me pause, imagining what it might be like. It's a good thought. I nod, while his thumb plays with my lips.

"I am going to miss these luscious lips of yours, Summer. And of course," Astor continues. "I'm crazy jealous that you're going to be in a house with two guys who are obviously in love with you, rather than with me."

What can I say to that? "I'm just happy being with you, Astor. And I'll see you sooner than you think."

Chapter 14

The next couple of weeks pass by in a blur. Aunt Sookie is pretty reluctant to take time off from her school, but she finally agrees to do it and concentrate on her recovery when my mother comes down to see her, taking her off on a trip to Palm Springs. Mom's eager to see her, and she's happy to see me again now I've been at Aunt Sookie's place for a while. She greets me with a big hug, asking me how I'm getting along there.

I find myself thinking of Astor, and of how well things are going with him. "I'm doing great, Mom. Just great."

I'm also *busy*. I told Aunt Sookie that I wouldn't have any problems covering her classes at the school while she takes time off work, but that means I'm there a *lot* in the next couple of weeks. There's a big difference between helping out with a class here and there, the way I was doing, and keeping up with the running of the school full time. Aunt Sookie had to be the first one there in the morning and the last one out of the school at night, which means that I have to do it while I'm filling in for her.

It's not so bad though. I actually enjoy teaching the classes, and not many people seem to have a problem with me doing it rather than my aunt. There's one older guy who starts complaining before one of the classes, coming up to me and demanding to know why Sookie isn't there, but I'm ready for that.

"She's had to take some time off," I say.

"And she thinks that it's acceptable to leave some girl in charge here?"

I shrug. "Yes, she does. Listen, how about this? Take the class as usual, and if you're not satisfied, then you don't have to pay for it or come to the next one."

"Well, that's fair, I guess," he says grudgingly.

It's actually a lot better than fair, but I leave that alone. I don't know what Aunt Sookie will say if I actually have to give the guy a free lesson. It doesn't work out like that though. I throw my all into a lesson on delivering monologues, with that idea of just taking the core of a character and saying it to the audience in that really authentic voice. By the end of it, the guy is ready to come up to me and pay all too willingly.

"I'm sorry I ever doubted you could do this," he says. "That was actually a very good lesson. Where did you learn to do that?"

How do I explain that I got most of it from years of playing dress-up with my aunt? I don't. So I just smile instead. "I guess it must run in the family."

The others are quick to help out with the school too, and they do pretty well. I guess that playing dress-up did a lot to help their acting skills too, and their confidence. Sometimes, Drew comes in and helps people to work on parts with muscular enthusiasm and plenty of energy. Sometimes, Nat does it, and he's more about careful preparation along with understanding the role on a deep level. Then there's Rachel, who is still pretty preoccupied with Ryan, but she's good at getting people to make different choices when it comes to seemingly obvious roles.

I love working with all of them. With Rachel, it's just having fun with my closest friend. With Drew and Nat... I have to admit, there are moments when that is harder. If we read through anything together, there's always that sense of tension there, like they want to do far more than just act with me. I know how they feel, just as I know how *I* feel. About Astor.

"How are things going with you and Astor?" Rachel asks me when I get back from my first weekend in North Carolina.

I smile just thinking about him. "It's so amazing being there with him, Rachel. We're getting so close. We talk about everything and anything. Sometimes we don't even have to say anything, but hold hands, and it feels so right."

"Has he..." Rachel doesn't finish that thought, but I know what she means.

"He's not putting any pressure on me," I say. "Honestly, there have been a few moments when I've been tempted, but Astor has backed off."

"That doesn't sound like most guys."

I shake my head. "Astor *isn't* most guys."

I don't even tell Rachel that there have been moments when I've been just a little worried, because I know how stupid it will sound. I *do* tell her about Lindsay New, the girl playing opposite him in the movie. She's a vision of blue eyed, blonde haired loveliness, with the kind of body that comes when you have a personal trainer following you around all day. And of course, she's very popular at the moment too.

"I think I hate her already," Rachel says.

I smile. "I thought you were over the whole 'pretty girls are mean' thing."

"Oh, don't tell me that she's nice as well," Rachel continues. "I don't think I could handle that too."

I shrug. "I haven't really seen enough of her to know. I mean, she's said hi when Astor is with me, but it's not like we're friends."

"And Astor?" Rachel asks. "Are he and Lindsay friends?"

It seems like she's cut through to exactly the problem. Astor and Lindsay *are* friends. They're close on set. I guess they have to be, since they're playing lovers in a movie with plenty of romance, but it can be hard seeing them talking together casually about lines or scenes and knowing that in some of those scenes, Astor is going to kiss her. I know it's just acting, but... well, it's hard to think about that happening when I'm not there. I'm only around the set on weekends, after all. I guess I just have to trust Astor.

Fourth of July comes around quickly, and we make plenty of preparations down at the beach house. Aunt Sookie is back from her trip with my mom, looking a lot better than she has been. She hugs me when she sees me and tells me what a great job I've been doing at her academy.

"It's been fun," I say.

She nods. "I'll bet it has. I have to admit, I'm looking forward to taking at least a few classes again. Oh, don't worry, I'm not going to do too much too fast, but I want to do *something*. I'm not good at sitting around."

I don't point out that what with trips to Palm Springs and everything else she does, Aunt Sookie isn't exactly sitting around. Instead, I just suggest that we could help get some food together for the barbeque we're having on the beach. So we end up at the same market where Nat, Drew and I bought so much food when we first got there. We fill a big cart with stuff for the evening, making sure that we also grab plenty of healthier options. That's one thing about Aunt Sookie's illness. We've all become more aware of what the food around us is like.

"How was Mrs. Donovan when you went to Palm Springs?" I ask Aunt Sookie while we shop for food.

She shakes her head. "Nadine didn't go."

"I thought you invited her down?"

"We did, but she couldn't make it, what with the divorce and everything. I guess…" Aunt Sookie shakes her head. "I guess it would have been nice if she could have made it, but she's been pretty down, with everything that's going on."

I guess she must be. It's a terrible situation, and it isn't good for Drew, Nat or Rachel either. They all seem pretty happy, and I guess it's good that they have somewhere like Aunt Sookie's place to go over the summer, but there are moments when I catch a glimpse of how hurt each of them is over the divorce and their father's infidelity.

It's easier not to think about that right then though. We're there to make sure that we have a great Fourth of July, and between us Aunt Sookie and I get all the food we're going to need for a real feast out on the beach. When we get back to the beach house, the others seem to be in the same party mood. Nat is working to get the barbeque together, Drew has taken charge of some fireworks, and Rachel is helping to get the area for the barbeque ready, with a little help from Ryan. I can see some of the looks Nat and Drew give him for being there. They still distrust him, although he seems to be a steady guy for Rachel, someone who she can lean on right now. Although he does not look the part, he seems like a great boyfriend right now for her. From the looks shared between Drew and Nat, I just hope that they can all keep from arguing. This is meant to be a happy occasion, after all.

Actually, for the first half hour or so, it *is* a happy occasion. Drew and Nat seem more relaxed around one another than they have been for a while, Aunt Sookie is talking to Ryan and Rachel, and I find myself enjoying the food from the barbeque while some of the neighbors on the beach come around to join in the celebration. I go over to see if Aunt Sookie wants anything from the barbeque.

Then her phone rings.

"Yes? Phillip? Why are you... what about Nadine?" Aunt Sookie listens to the caller, who seems to be Mr. Donovan, for several seconds. From the way the color drains from her face, I know it isn't good news.

"What?" Rachel says. "Is there something wrong with Mom?"

Aunt Sookie actually ignores her. That, even more than the rest of it, tells me how serious this is.

"You're sure?" she says. "No, I mean, it couldn't have been an accident or something? No, of *course* I'm not saying that, it's just that I never expected... No, well, we all know why that is, don't we? Yes, you too. Goodbye, Phillip."

Aunt Sookie hangs up, looking furious for several seconds as she just stands there. Cautiously, almost tentatively, I reach out to touch her arm.

"Aunt Sookie, what's happened? What's wrong?"

She starts, as though only just remembering that I'm there. "I need to talk to you, Drew, Nat and Rachel, inside now."

"What is it?" Rachel asks. "Did something happen to Mom? I want to know!"

"Rachel, I'll tell you inside."

Rachel shakes her head. She looks utterly terrified, as though she can't quite believe what is happening. "Tell me now. If something has happened to Mom, I have a right to know."

Aunt Sookie winces. "Your mother took an overdose of sleeping pills. She's in the hospital."

"In the hospital? Sleeping pills?" Rachel sounds like she doesn't understand any of it. I put an arm around her, trying to comfort her even though I don't understand it any better than she does.

"How could that happen," Rachel demands.

Aunt Sookie looks pointedly at Ryan. "I really don't think…"

"*How?*"

"They think she took them deliberately, Rachel," Aunt Sookie says gently. "They think that your mother was trying to kill herself."

Chapter 15

Rachel stands there for several seconds. Then she just screams and rushes forward, knocking a whole pile of barbeque things to the ground. I've never seen her that upset before. I start to go to her, but Ryan beats me to it. Rachel looks like she might spin around and hit him, but Ryan pulls her close and leads her away towards the house, talking softly.

That leaves Drew and Nat. Drew's expression is grim, so hard and set I know that there has to be far more going on under the surface. Nat looks worse though. His skin is ashen, and he looks like he can barely stand up. I go to him without thinking, wrapping my arms around him even though Drew looks at me like he can't believe I'm doing it. Aunt Sookie moves to hug him, squeezing him tightly while I hold onto Nat. I guess in that moment, we all need some comfort.

"I have to go to her," Nat whispers, sharply and suddenly. "I should never have come here. She needs me back there."

He pulls back from me, rushing towards the house. I follow as he heads upstairs to the room he's sharing with Drew and pulls out a bag, starting to throw things into it.

"Nat, what are you doing?"

"Packing. I have to go. I have to get back there."

I think I understand. I reach out for his shoulder. "Nat, I'm so sorry. I know how much your mom means to you. If there's anything I can do…"

Nat looks at me. He looks shocked, and worse. He looks like he's on the brink of breaking down completely. "Summer, don't you see? Mom sent us here so that she could do this. All that time I thought that she was trying to give us some space away from the divorce… she was going to do this."

He sits down on the bed, his head in his hands. I sit beside him, holding onto him.

"You don't know that for sure, Nat," I say. "And the important thing is that she didn't succeed. Your dad found her in time. She's going to be fine."

Nat's head is still in his hands, and as I gently peel his hands away from his face, I can see the tears streaming from his eyes. Nat is crying, making no attempt to disguise it, his eyes red from it.

"This is my fault, Summer."

"No," I say, "it isn't."

"I should have told her earlier about Dad, so maybe they could have worked it out. Or I should have just not told her at all, because then it wouldn't have hurt her. I could have talked to Dad, confronted him. I could have gotten him to stop seeing that... that *slut* secretary of his..."

"Nat," I say gently, "this isn't helping, and it's not your fault. Don't even blame yourself for this. Your mother is a grown woman. She knew what she was doing. Your father, too. It's not up to you what happens between them."

I've never seen him like this before. He's so hurt right now. So vulnerable. I hold him tightly, wishing that I could take away some of that pain, and his arms tighten around me. Then he's kissing me, quickly, almost furiously, like it's the most natural thing for us to do, and I kiss him back the same way, fueled by all the hurt and pain he's going through. I don't know how long we spend wrapped around each other, his lips kissing every square inch of my face until both his hands are holding my face, and he has his lips on mine, still filled with passion. It just seems to make sense in that moment, the raw emotion of everything we feel coming out like that. And not just the emotion of this moment. It's the emotion of all those moments we've had to bottle up something we've felt about one another, coming out in a tidal wave that sweeps us along as we kiss for a long time.

When we pull apart, Nat still has my face in his hands. "You've always been my summer." His fingers caress my face, making me look at him with longing. I shake my head to clear it. Why does Nat still have that effect on me?

"Nat," I begin, "I…"

Nat lets go of me. "Don't say it. Whatever it is, please don't say it. I don't know what just happened, and I'm glad it did, but… now is just the worst time for it to happen."

I stare at him, trying to make sense of it. "What? Why?"

Nat shakes his head. "Because I still have to leave here, Summer."

I pause, looking at the bag he's started to pack and feeling guilty that I'd forgotten. Feeling guilty for having kissed him like that too, when his mom…

"I have to go back to San Francisco," he says. "My mom needs me there."

"Nat…" I begin, trying to think of a way to talk him out of this. It feels like he's blaming himself for all this when he shouldn't. He can't.

"I'm the eldest," Nat says, "so I should have been watching out for her. I should have known Mom might try this. Look, don't tell the twins this, okay?"

"Tell them what?"

Nat looks down. "Mom has been depressed for a while now. She suffers bouts of it, and she's been on medication to try to help. But it obviously hasn't... oh, I should have been there."

"You couldn't have known," I say.

"I could have," Nat insists. "I should have. And Dad... he's been such an ass about this whole thing. It's like he couldn't care less about Mom or any of us."

"I can come with you to San Francisco." I say it before I can stop myself. Nat needs me, and I need him right then. After everything he's told me, I don't just want to let him go. "I don't want you to handle this alone."

"No, Summer," Nat says. He holds me again briefly, and it's such a gentle, fleeting touch. "I can't deal with you there while I'm having to deal with my mother and father, their nasty divorce, having to deal with the details of Mom's care. I know I've told you that I have feelings for you, and I do, but this… I have to focus on this right now. I don't think I'd be able to do that if you were there. Not the way I should."

"So I'd just be a distraction?" I say.

"Don't be angry," Nat says. "I'm just trying to do what's right here, Summer. Anyway, you have your aunt to worry about, with her condition."

"It isn't as serious as what your mom's going through."

"But she still needs you," Nat insists, with a serious expression that tells me I'm not going to win this argument. He stands up, heading for his bag. "I'm sorry, Summer."

My heart falls, and I can hear it shatter. Rejected by him again. It doesn't help that I can understand why he's done it. It just hurts that he has. "All right, Nat. I hope you'll be okay."

I walk out of there before Nat can see just how hurt I am. This isn't about me. This is about his mom. I walk out of there so fast I don't even see Drew until I walk straight into him. He catches hold of me, steadying me and folding me into his arms.

"Whoa, Summer," he says, brushing away tears I hadn't known had fallen from my eyes. "It's going to be okay. Mom's going to be fine. Your mom is going over to San Francisco now to be there. Aunt Sookie would have gone too, but with her being unwell…"

No, it makes sense that my mom should go. "Nat's going too," I manage to say. "Are you? I mean, I know you must want to."

Drew's worried expression is back. "I should, but I think someone should stay here too. I'm worried about Sookie. She still isn't looking too good, and everyone else is going to San Francisco, so maybe I should stay."

"Everyone is going?" I ask.

Drew nods. "Rachel calmed down after a while, and she's going to head out with Nat. Ryan's going too, which is kind of good of him." Drew sounds surprised by that. I guess the boy who slept with his sister is turning out to be a lot better person than he expected. "I don't want to leave Sookie alone."

"I'll still be here," I say.

"Then I don't want you and Sookie left here with no one else," Drew replies. He sighs. "I want to see Mom, but she has so many people going there to be with her, and I'm not even sure what I would say. I think I'm better staying here with the two of you. Here… well, I can be whatever you need."

He holds me tight then, pressing me against the strong expanse of his chest. His hand strokes the back of my hair as he holds me, and though it probably looks like he's comforting me, I guess that Drew is getting as much comfort out of this as I am. At least until Nat walks out of his room, his bag in his hand.

I pull back from Drew instinctively, looking from him to Nat. I can feel the tension there, and maybe the anger, but neither of them says anything about it. I guess it isn't the thing that's uppermost in their minds right then.

"Take care of Summer and Sookie, bro," Nat says after a second or two. It's so coldly practical, like the way he pushed me away from him. "I have to go. Mom will expect it."

"Is your flight booked?" Drew asks. Obviously, they're trying to do the guy thing of not showing how they feel.

Nat nods. "I phoned Dad and he's sending the company's private jet. He told the Board that it was an emergency, apparently." I see his jaw clench for a moment or two. "It takes Mom trying to kill herself before he thinks of any of us as an emergency."

"Rachel and Ryan are both going too," Drew says.

"Both of them?"

Drew nods. "I think Ryan drove her to his place so he could grab some things, but if you text Rachel and let her know to meet you at the air field, they can go there. Summer's mom is going to meet you and fly out too. You know how close she, Sookie and Mom are."

"I'll call Mom to let her know where to meet you, Nat," I say, realizing that I should be trying to help here. "Unless you want to wait here for her and go together? Drew and I can take you and Mom there."

Kailin Gow

Nat's eyes rove over me for several seconds before he looks at Drew. He seems to relax a little. Just a little, but it's enough. "All right."

I walk past him to get my phone, fetching it from my room and keeping an eye on the two boys while I do it. Nat is trying to be so strong standing there. So strong that it makes him seem almost hard and cold. Especially with the way he refused to let me follow him to San Francisco. Drew is all passion and feeling, looking over at me while I make the call to my mom to tell her where to meet us. Even now, with everything that's going on, he isn't able to disguise the way he looks at me.

Why should I care? Why should it matter to me that either of them wants me? I'm with Astor. I'm *happy* with Astor. That should be enough for me, yet I can't stop myself from thinking about them. Astor is a long way away, while Nat and Drew are here now, and they are both enough to make my heart beat faster. Of course, soon, Nat won't be here. It will just be me, Drew and Aunt Sookie in the house.

Chapter 16

The next few days without Rachel and Nat in the house seem strange. I've gotten used to them being there, like we're all one big family. The thought of them having to leave because of problems with their real family feels surreal, like it shouldn't be happening. Of course, it shouldn't. None of them should have to deal with all the things they're dealing with right now.

I get texts from Rachel pretty regularly, telling me how things are going. She's upset by it all, but I notice how much she mentions Ryan too. He's always taking her off to the movies, or out for a walk, or something else that manages to distract her from the worst of it. She doesn't talk much about her mom, or about Nat, though. That kind of worries me a little. Are things that bad with them?

I'd kind of expected Drew to be more withdrawn without the others there, especially given the whole situation. Yet somehow, he's the total opposite. The morning after his brother and sister leave, he goes running with me as usual, up the beach and back again. Then he makes breakfast, being sure it fits in with Aunt Sookie's new diet.

It's hard adjusting to my aunt's situation. She's obviously worried about Mrs. Donovan, who's her friend, and I think she blames herself a little for not talking her into going away with them. At the same time though, she has her own health to think about, getting the balance of her diet and her life right so that she can control her condition. It looks like the operation might have worked, but Aunt Sookie is still careful about what she does. More careful than I've ever seen her, in fact. It's like the combination of her illness and hearing about Mrs. Donovan has scared her away from living life the way she always used to.

Loving Summer (Loving Summer Series #1)

Drew seems to be making such an effort with Aunt Sookie. He helps me to take some of her classes at her academy, but he's also there to help her get back into teaching her own classes, and his cooking repertoire quickly expands to take in the restrictions of Aunt Sookie's diet. It's like the fact that he can't go to be with his mom has somehow spurred him on to be even more responsible here.

Not that it's all about responsibility with Drew. He still runs with me, and he spends most of the rest of the time with me too. With Astor away filming, and both Rachel and Nat gone for now, there's really only the two of us. So we quickly become inseparable. Whatever I'm doing, whether it's helping Aunt Sookie, going to the library, heading down to the store or just watching TV, Drew's there making me smile. He's always there to play games with me, or to chase me down the beach laughing, or to bring me a flower from some new hidden spot he has found, which he then goes on to show me. It's like he can't bear for me to be unhappy.

Or maybe it's just that *he* doesn't want to be unhappy. Maybe by doing all this, he can take his mind off what's happening with his mom and dad. Or maybe it's even simpler than that. Maybe this is just Drew finally being himself without his brother and sister around. It's hard to tell which answer is the right one, here. I know one thing it isn't, though. It isn't the thing I kind of fear it might be when Drew first starts being so nice. I'm worried that with Nat and Astor gone, he's simply trying to make a move on me. Yet that's one thing he doesn't do. He doesn't try to kiss me. Doesn't try to pressure me into being his girlfriend, or into sleeping with him the way so many other girls have. He's just *there*, as a friend, as someone who I can talk to, whom he can talk to, to hold hands and walk on the beach with, to run with, to sit together and watch the sun set. There are times when we go swimming, too. He wears swim trunks instead of his boxers like the first day, and it's like we were ten years old again, splashing and chasing each other in the pool. But when he catches me and holds me, all I can feel and think about is his warm skin against mine, and how when we look into each other's eyes, we can't seem to stop looking.

The others aren't there in the same way. They can't be. Astor is still caught up in filming with Lindsay, and the next time I go out there, he has to re-shoot several scenes so that we don't get to see as much of one another as I would like. At least one of those scenes involves kissing her. Even though it's just acting, it's hard watching the two of them like that. It's even harder when Astor kisses me straight afterwards. It's obviously intended to show me that it's still me he cares about in real life, but it's like I can taste Lindsay on his lips as we kiss. When I'm there, though, he goes out of his way to spend time with me, cuddling with me and holding me while we fall asleep on his bed, his fingers entwined in mine. It's sweet, but at the same time, I can sense how much he wants to take our relationship further. I know he's sincere, but the way the film is going and how he has to do intense intimate scenes now with Lindsay, I can't help thinking if any of it is real.

Rachel calls most days, but it's more than a week before Nat calls me, phoning me one afternoon while I'm out on the beach.

"Hi Summer," he says, his voice deep, warm, and soft like velvet.

"Nat." I can't help smiling at the sound of his voice. "It seems like forever since I last heard from you."

"I didn't…" Nat pauses. "I wanted to be sure about what I was going to say before I said it. I wanted to concentrate on things here."

"How's your mom?" I ask. That's one thing Rachel hasn't told me much about. She gets upset when it comes up, like it's too hard for her. I've gotten into the habit of being a distraction from it all, talking about things that don't matter.

"She's better than she was," Nat says. "She's out of the hospital, over the physical effects of the overdose. Now though… there's still so much to deal with."

"Like the divorce," I say.

"No. Dad at least cares enough not to take advantage of this with the divorce proceedings," Nat says. "He's called a halt to them for now. What happens after that… well, I guess it's up to Mom when she's feeling well enough to deal with it."

"You're making it sound like this is going to take a *long* time," I reply.

Nat sighs. "I think it probably will. Depression… it isn't just what Dad did, Summer. My mother has been depressed most of her life, so dealing with this… I guess it won't ever be over. Not really."

I can hear how saddened he is by that thought. He sounds like he's still blaming himself for it. How many times can I tell Nat that it isn't up to him? I don't think he'll believe it any more now than he did before he left.

"Nat, the important thing is that you're doing the best you can."

"It just doesn't feel like it's enough some days, you know?"

I kind of do know. I know it every time I see Aunt Sookie looking a little tired or run down by her day. I know it every time she insists to keep on going despite that.

"I've missed you," Nat says softly like he's hanging onto every word. The words come out of nowhere, catching me completely off guard. I guess I should have expected them somewhere, after everything we said to one another before he left, but they still take me by surprise.

"I've missed you too," I say. It's the truth. I've thought about Nat just about every day since he's left. Even on those days when I've been visiting Astor. I guess crushes that have lasted for years don't go away that easily.

"I wish you could have come up to San Francisco with me," he says. His voice sounds raw, like he's having a hard time saying it. There is so much emotion in it, so much meaning, I can feel it thick around me. Then I remember how he broke my heart again that day, after that passionate kiss, the kiss we'd been waiting all our lives to have.

That makes me just a little angry. "I offered. You turned me down."

"I couldn't…" Nat pauses. "I had to focus on Mom. But I haven't been able to stop thinking about you." He pauses and then he groans, and I imagine him running his hand through his messy copper hair. "Oh Summer. Maybe I shouldn't be telling you this, but I don't care. I've been keeping this to myself for so long. I want you to know that I've been thinking about what could have happened after we kissed."

"So you're suddenly saying that you want us to be together again?" I ask, still annoyed with him, even though there's a part of me that is hoping more than anything that Nat will say yes.

"I… I think the problems are still there," Nat says. "I'm not coming back to Malibu, Summer. I'm going to stay in San Francisco and take a job with my father's company. I'm going to be a part of it while I attend Stanford next year, while you're going to be in Malibu with your aunt, and I know that you can't run out on her at the moment. It can't work, Summer."

"So you've raised my hopes again just so that you can squash them?" I demand.

"No, it's not like that," Nat says. "I care about you, Summer. I really do. If I could think of a way to make this work, then I would. Please believe me. It's just that I don't think it *can* work right now between us. I'm sorry."

I bite back tears, feeling like I did three years ago the last time I saw him before his family moved. He made it seem like he would keep in touch with me, that he would try to come back to visit, if only he can find a way. He never did find his way back to Aunt Sookie's until only this summer. "I'm sorry, too, Nat," I say. "I'm sorry you don't have the guts to go after what you want, even when what you want is there right in front of you. I'm sorry you seem to want to protect me from those who you think will hurt me, when just by telling me you care for me, and then go around to tell me we can't be together, you've hurt me more than anyone you've tried to protect me against." I take a deep breath, and my tears flow freely now down my cheeks. "I'm sorry I ever had a crush on you."

He hangs up, and I only just stop myself from throwing the phone out into the surf. Yet again, it feels like Nat has trampled on my feelings, playing with me and never letting me get what I really want. Just one real acknowledgement that we could be together. I try wiping away my tears as I start to walk back towards the house.

Drew meets me at the door, and when he sees the phone in my hand, and my cheeks, probably still wet from the few tears that escaped, he puts a hand on my shoulder.

"Summer, what is it?"

"Nat called," I say, trying not to sound like it matters. I obviously don't do it well.

Drew's face stills. "And let me guess, he pulled you around for a while before telling you that you couldn't ever be together, but that he really cared about you anyway so that there might just be a chance." Drew sounds even angrier than I am.

"It doesn't matter, Drew," I say.

He shakes his head. "It matters to me. If it weren't for Nat, and that crush of yours that somehow manages to survive everything he does to you…" He sighs, pulling me into his broad chest to hold me, while gently stroking my back. "Summer, he's my brother, and I love him, but he's being such a…" Drew can't finish, he's so angry. "Come on. I guess we could both do with a run right now."

We run, just there and then as we are, not even bothering to get changed for it. I run without trying to pace myself, just running flat out up the beach with my hair streaming behind me. Drew runs like he's chasing me, and together we sprint along the sand at the kind of speed we don't normally go near in our more measured morning runs. It's what I need after a call like that from Nat. Just something that can let me turn my frustration into something raw and physical. Something simple.

I run until I'm almost ready to collapse, then sit on the sand. Drew is there beside me, breathing as heavily as I am, sucking air into his lungs in great heaves that match mine. He sits beside me there on the sand, looking out at the ocean. We don't kiss. We certainly don't do anything else. We don't even speak right then, and I guess that we don't need to. We just sit there inches from one another, together. After a minute or so Drew slides his hand into mine, but that's it.

We sit there staring out over the water until the sun starts to set. By that time, we're both breathing normally, and the cooler evening air makes me wish that I'd taken the time to put on jogging gear before running. They're such normal concerns that they hardly seem right then, but they're reminders that we can't sit there forever.

Still, we manage a little while longer, and he covers me up with his sweatshirt, which he gently slips over me. The golden orange of the sun setting over the waters casts a glow on Drew's smooth tanned skin and his handsome features. That's when I realize how Drew really is beautiful, inside and out.

Chapter 17

<u>Drew</u>

Sitting next to Summer is hard. No, that isn't right. *Just* sitting next to Summer is hard. It would be easy if I could reach out and crush her to me. It would be easy if I could kiss her, and hold her, and slide her down on the sand next to me…

But I can't. I have to sit there watching the ocean with her, aware of every breath she takes. Aware of the sexy sheen of sweat on her skin after that breakneck run, so that she seems to gleam in the fading sunlight. If she were any other girl, I wouldn't hesitate, but she isn't. She's Summer. I love her more than any other girl I've ever met, and kissing her isn't like kissing another girl. It isn't casual.

It means something. It means the world to me. That's why I can't do it.

Part of the reason, anyway. I stand up, brushing sand from my jeans as I think about Nat. He's my brother, and I love him, but what he's doing to Summer isn't right. He's stringing her along, playing with her heart the way a cat plays with a piece of string, batting it this way and that until he gets bored. If he were here, I think I'd probably knock some sense into him for that. He can't treat Summer like that.

But he isn't here, is he? He's with Mom, doing the responsible thing. He and Rachel, so that I'm here with Summer and Sookie. I want to believe that I stayed because of Sookie, because she needs the extra help while she's adjusting to her diabetes. Maybe it's even true. There's part of me though that keeps asking if that's the real reason I stayed. Did I stay here rather than going to look after my own mother because I really wanted to help that much? Did I maybe do it because I was scared of going back to the house and seeing Mom or Dad, not knowing what to say to them?

Or did I do it because I knew Summer would be here? Did I do it because her precious Astor is away, and I'd be alone in the house with her and Sookie? No. No, I won't believe I did it just for that. I want her. I'll admit that. I want her more than anything, but I didn't just stay here to be with her. As if to prove it, I force myself to help Summer back to her feet, giving her the lightest of pecks on her cheek.

"What was that for?" she asks, smiling.

"It just seemed like the right thing to do," I reply. "A bit like this run. Are you feeling better now?"

She nods. "How is it that you always know what to do to cheer me up?"

I shrug, not wanting to give her the real answer, which is simply that I love her. "I guess I just know you that well. Now, we should probably get back for dinner."

"Actually," Summer says. "I'm taking one of the evening classes today. You know, for people who want to do them after work? I'm going to take it, and then drive back with Aunt Sookie, so can you maybe drive me over there?"

"Okay," I say. "Race you back to the house, then?"

We run back, and Summer quickly showers and changes before we head out. It feels strange, driving her car with her as a passenger, because so far this summer, she's mostly been the one driving me. It feels good to finally be in control.

"I don't know what I'd do without you, Drew," Summer says as we pull up outside the school.

"You'd probably just take the bus."

"No," she replies, and when she reaches out to touch my arm, that contact is almost electric. "I mean it. With you staying here to help, even with everything that's going on… not many people would have done that, Drew. I appreciate it."

I know she does, and her smile is beautiful, but right then, I wish that Summer "appreciated" things in the same way some of the girls I've been with this summer did. God knows how much I want her…so much that it hurts. I wince at that thought. I want more than that with Summer, though. So much more, yet sometimes it's hard to stop thinking the way I'm so used to thinking about girls. I know I can't treat her like that.

Nat can't go on treating Summer the way he has been, either. In fact, just the thought of it makes anger bubble up in me again, so that once she's disappeared into the school, I hang around in the parking lot so that I have the time to take out my phone and call Nat. He answers quickly.

"Drew? If you're calling for another update about Mom, I don't have much else to tell you. Everything's the way it was yesterday. Oh, and Rachel has gone out with Ryan and Dad. I think he wants to know what kind of boy is hanging around with his daughter. It's nice to know he can take an interest *some* of the time."

I start to agree with him, but stop myself. This isn't about Rachel, and it isn't about our father. "Nat," I say, "I want to talk to you about Summer."

"What about her?" I can hear the change in Nat's tone instantly, like he's wary; worried about what I might say. I guess he has a reason to be right now.

"What about her?" I say, echoing him. "Nat, you need to stop playing games with her. You really upset her earlier."

"I didn't mean to," Nat replies, "but what am I supposed to do?"

"That's simple. You should stop messing her around. You know that she's loved you practically forever. If you love her, then say it to her. Be with her. If not, you need to stop stringing her along with this idea that you might love her one day, or that it's just the circumstances that are making things difficult."

"Because *you* know so much about relationships," Nat shoots back. I slam my hand into the dashboard hard.

"This isn't about me, Nat. This is about what you're doing to Summer. If you don't want her; if you can't be with her, just say it. Say it and let her go. Stop hurting her by never making things final."

There's a pause, and when Nat speaks again, his voice is hurt. "I want to. I want things to be that simple, but I can't just let her go. I *can't*. She brings back every good memory I've ever had. She's all those summers we had together. And now... well, just being around her makes things better."

"I know that," I say. How can he think I don't know that? I see it every time Summer walks into a room. I *feel* it every time she's close. "You think I don't feel exactly the same way? The difference is that she actually wants you. She's wanted you since we were just kids, and yet you keep trampling on her feelings. It isn't fair for her, Nat."

"You think it would be fair to get her caught up in everything that's going on right now instead, especially when she has enough she has to deal with?" Nat demands, raising his voice slightly. "Oh, it's always so easy for you, isn't it? You *and* Rachel. You two aren't the ones Dad puts so much pressure on to take over his company when he's ready to retire. You aren't the one Mom relies on to do all the things that Dad is meant to be doing. You aren't the ones who have to make sure that everything turns out okay with her. I mean, you didn't even come back here."

I bite back my anger for a moment or two, remembering that this isn't about me. "That still doesn't give you the right to make things harder for Summer, Nat. It doesn't let you mess her around."

Nat doesn't say anything for several seconds. In fact, by the time he speaks again, I've started to think that he might have hung up.

"Okay," he says, "you're right. I shouldn't go back and forth with Summer. I shouldn't get her hopes up when right now, I can't even let myself think about her. It's over with her. I'm not going to try to hold her back. I guess that makes you happy, Drew?"

I can hear the resentment there. He knows that without him in the way, I'm going to try to get closer to Summer, and I can't exactly deny it, because it's true.

"It must be easy, not having any responsibilities," Nat says suddenly.

That's enough to make me react. "Nat, I'm planning to go back to help with Mom as soon as I can. You know that I stayed here so that I could help Sookie keep her school running while she's sick. As for the hard time that you're constantly talking about Dad giving you, remember that he's pretty hard on me too."

"Hard? You've always been his favorite. The big football star."

"And football is *his* dream for me, not mine. You've seen all the time I have to put into training because he has some crazy idea about me playing in the NFL. Okay, so I like to play a little, but he's the reason I have to take it seriously. So don't try to tell me that you're the only one he puts pressure on."

At that moment, Summer steps out of the school, standing lit by the glow of the acting academy's doorway in the pale sundress she changed into after our run. I can see the outline of her body in her barely there dress, and every part of me wants her then. She looks… incredible. It's hard not to just hang up and go running over there to snatch her into my arms. Instead, I have to keep talking to my brother.

"You're sure about Summer?" I ask him. I don't want Nat turning around and changing his mind a week from now. That would only hurt Summer more. Not to mention what it would do to any chance I have with her. I can compete with a lot of things, but a whole lifetime's worth of crush isn't one of them. I want this *clear*.

Nat hesitates again, and in that hesitation, I watch Summer. For a second or two she's standing there, talking to someone inside, laughing at something. She's beautiful when she laughs. The whole world is beautiful when she laughs, like it's a better place just because she's happy. Maybe it even is. Finally, though, Nat speaks.

"I can't handle a relationship with any girl right now, let alone a long distance one."

That's what I was hoping to hear. Okay, so I feel a little bad for Nat, but he's had his chance with Summer. In fact, he's had plenty of chances. He could have said yes to her at any point since we were kids, and they would have been together. He could have said yes to her after we showed up here in Malibu, and again, instant happy ever after. He didn't. Instead, he chose to jerk Summer's feelings around and never deal with anything. Now it's my turn.

"Well," I say, "I guess that's the closest thing I'm going to get to your blessing, right Nat?"

He starts to say something but I hang up. Right then, I'm not interested in my brother. I'm interested in Summer, and she's heading my way.

Chapter 18

<u>Summer</u>

Drew is surprisingly kind for the next day or so. It's not just the things he does, because he has dinner waiting for me and Aunt Sookie most nights, and he goes running with me as usual in the morning. It's more the way he does them, like he's making a special effort to be attentive. He even drives me and Aunt Sookie back from her academy after work the next day, and heads over to the local supermarket with us to pick up groceries.

He cooks dinner, while somehow managing to keep up a simultaneous three-way game of poker with me and Aunt Sookie, who is winning easily. When I ask her how, she smiles.

"I got a lot of practice in when I was in Vegas in my twenties."

"What were you doing in Vegas?"

Aunt Sookie shakes her head. "Let's just say that things got a little wild and leave it at that, yes?"

That sounds like the kind of story Drew and I are going to have to get out of her over the next hour or two. It's strange to think sometimes that Aunt Sookie is only in her thirties. She's done so much, and seen so much, that it's like she's lived twice that long in terms of her experiences. Or maybe it's just that she seems older right now. I'm starting to think that her operation hasn't helped as much as the doctors thought it might. She's looking drawn tonight. Almost grey. Maybe she went back to work a little soon.

"I'm just going to go lie down," she says, almost as soon as we're done eating. "It's been a long day."

It makes me cry to see my aunt like that. She's so young, and she should be so full of life, yet it seems that her condition has just sucked that life right out of her. I feel Drew's arm around me as he takes me through to the lounge, sitting me down on the sofa and holding me, just letting me cry.

"It's going to be all right, Summer."

I cling onto him there, and he gently brushes away my tears with his thumb. That same thumb brushes my lips and I taste the saltiness of my tears, then look up at him, knowing what I want from him in that moment. He's just inches away from me. Close enough that we could easily...

My phone goes off, and I start, pulling back from Drew as I realize what I almost did just then. I answer my phone, and a quick wave of guilt bursts through me, because it's Astor. Astor, who's meant to be my boyfriend. Astor, about whom I should be thinking constantly.

Astor, who has just spent most of the last few weeks kissing Lindsay New.

"Astor?"

"Summer, it's good to hear your voice. Listen, I'm not far away. I just wanted to check that you were home."

"Yes. Yes, I am." I can hear the happiness in my own voice as I say that. Astor is coming here. He's back.

"Then I'll be there in just a few minutes. I can't wait to see you."

"Me too."

"I have things I want to tell you, too."

He leaves it at that, and my heart leaps at the thought of him coming here. He's been so busy that I've barely heard from him when I haven't actually been in North Carolina with him. Just a few texts to tell me how much he's missing me, and how he hopes to see me again soon.

I look over at Drew, who's still sitting near me on the couch. He doesn't look happy. I can guess why. We were so close to taking things further. To being far more than just friends. I think… I think I might even have slept with him, if Astor hadn't interrupted. Yet now, looking at it with Astor on his way, I'm not sure that I want us to be more than friends. Which is a problem, because Drew has openly told me that he can't just be friends with me.

"That was Astor," I say.

Drew takes a deep breath. "I heard. Summer…"

"He said that he has something to tell me," I continue, cutting Drew off. I don't want to give him the chance to have this argument.

"Do you know what he wants to tell you?" Drew asks. He looks like he wants to say far more, but he's obviously guessed that I'm not going to let him go there.

I shrug, and try to ignore the way Drew watches my body moving as I do it. "I haven't even heard from Astor in days, Drew. It could be anything."

I stand, but Drew stands with me, reaching out to grip my upper arms so that I'm forced to look at him.

"Summer, I've been wanting to tell you something too. For a long time. I figured I finally could now that Nat isn't…"

"Nat isn't what?" I ask. "Drew, what does any of this have to do with Nat?"

Drew shakes his head. "Look Summer. I know how you feel about Nat. We all do. You've been feeling that way for him for years, and I know part of you still feels that way, but Nat… Nat can't handle a relationship with anyone right now. It just isn't going to happen. You have to move on."

"Nat told you that?" I ask.

Drew nods. "I know my brother too. I know what he's going through, and he's trying for a complete break from everything here. You're just going to make yourself unhappy if you keep going after him. Whereas for me... well, you've always been the girl for me, Summer."

I blink as he says that. I know he means it. He's said it before, but I thought we'd dealt with it. "Drew, that isn't going to happen. We're friends. I hope we'll stay friends, but I can't be more than that for you. Rachel would kill us, for one thing."

"This has nothing to do with Rachel," Drew says, his expression growing more serious. "All this summer, with you around, it has been the best time of my life. I've changed because of it. I'm not running around after girls like I was, because every time I touch one, I find myself thinking of you, and how meaningless anything with any girl who *isn't* you is. Yes, we're friends, but that just makes it worse, because it means we're that much closer. You're even closer to me than my sister, these days. That has to count for..."

The doorbell rings, and I'm so grateful for it as I rush over to the door. At the same time Aunt Sookie calls out from the bedroom, asking for water. Drew hurries into the kitchen for it, while I go to the door to let Astor in.

He's standing there with a big bouquet of roses in his hand, dressed casually in jeans and a t-shirt featuring some band whose "world tour" doesn't seem to have gotten further than North Carolina. He looks amazing, with his short blonde hair seeming to glow in the sun, and his smile cutting right through to my heart. He steps inside, puts the flowers down and pulls me into a lingering kiss, all in one movement. He kisses me like a starving man, and it's a long time before we come up for air.

"Summer," Astor says, holding me at arm's length so that he can look at me. "God, I've missed you. Your touch, everything…"

I smile back at him. "I've missed you too, but why rush over here like this? I could have met you at the airport."

He kisses me again then. "I wanted it to be at least a little bit of a surprise." He looks a little more serious then.

"Besides, with how sick your aunt is, and how much you've been doing, I thought that someone should be here to take care of *you*."

I have to admit that sounds good. "Doesn't this mean you're missing shooting time?"

Astor shakes his head. "I have a break today and tomorrow. I thought about all the places I could spend that break, and frankly, the only one I cared about was here, in your arms. I'm crazy about you, you know."

I laugh at that, because it just doesn't sound like the kind of thing normal guys say. "That's good. I was starting to get worried that you might have fallen in love with Lindsay."

Astor pulls back. "You've really been worried about that? Had I've known, I would have introduced you to Lindsay's boyfriend the last time you were on set."

"Her boyfriend?"

Astor nods. "Leo. He's from Dallas, and from what I hear, they're pretty serious. It's one reason Lindsay was as worried about the kissing scenes as I was."

"Oh." It's all I can think of to say.

Astor takes my hand. "Summer, you had me going nuts for days. You haven't been returning my emails or calls. Was that what it was about?"

I hadn't even realized that I'd missed any from him. Have I been that distracted by Aunt Sookie and the classes I'm running for her at the school? Have I been that distracted by Drew? "I guess I haven't checked my messages that often. I'm sorry."

Astor puts an arm around me, leading me out of the beach house. His car is there, and he opens the passenger side. "I have something for you."

There's another ribbon-wrapped Tiffany's box on the seat. Astor lets go of me long enough to reach in and pick it up, pressing it into my hands. I shake my head even before I touch it.

"It's too much," I say.

"You don't even know what it is yet," Astor points out. "I think we've had this discussion before, too. I want to do this, Summer. Now, are you going to open that box, or should I do it?"

In the end, he does it, showing what sits within. It's a silver bracelet with a silver heart on it, and I can see the inscription there. It reads *I love you, A.* It's beautiful.

"Do you like it?" Astor asks.

"It's lovely," I say, kissing him.

"I'm glad you like it." There's just a hint of disappointment in his voice. "What about the message?"

I reach up to touch his face. "You make me happy, Astor. Happier than anyone else could."

That seems to please Astor. "Good. I was thinking of you all the time we were filming, you know. That's how I was able to make the role seem real when it came to anything romantic. I thought about you, and how much I cared about you. I thought about what it would be like if you were there. I love you, Summer."

This kiss is his most passionate yet, and it leaves me breathless. When Astor finally pulls back, he stares at me with intense eyes. He isn't the only one. Drew is standing at the door to the beach house, looking out at us. He looks jealous, but I know it's more than that, because he looks almost… frightened, too.

"Drew? What is it?"

"It's Sookie," he says. "She passed out. I've called 911, but I'm not sure what else to do. I think she needs to go to the emergency room."

Chapter 19

We travel with Aunt Sookie to the hospital, following behind the ambulance. By the time we get there, the doctors are already working on her. One, a woman who looks almost too young to be a doctor, comes over to talk to us.

"Hi, I'm Doctor Hungerford. You're Ms. Jones' family?"

"I'm her niece," I say. "Other than me, I guess her closest family is my mom, her sister."

Doctor Hungerford nods, looking serious. "Right now, your aunt is in a diabetic coma, specifically what we call a nonketotic hyperosmolar coma. It's brought about through a combination of dehydration and insulin imbalance, and I have to warn you that it can be quite dangerous if not dealt with quickly."

"But you *are* dealing with it?" Astor asks, moving to stand beside me.

"We're working to bring Ms. Jones out of the coma, yes," Doctor Hungerford says.

"There's something else, isn't there?" Drew says. "What is it?"

The doctor looks to each of them, then to me. "I'm not really comfortable…"

"Please just tell me," I say.

She nods. "Your aunt's condition is serious. Normally, we would expect to see this type of coma only in more advanced diabetes patients, and reading her notes, it suggests that the operation she had has failed. That means that she could be open to all the kinds of complications that come with the disease. At the moment, we're particularly worried about the pressure this state puts on her heart, and the possibility of vascular compromise."

"You mean that Aunt Sookie could have a heart attack?" I ask.

The doctor looks at me for a second or two, then nods. "We're going to do everything we can to help her, though."

A lot happens quickly after that, but I don't get to see most of it. The doctors keep working on my aunt, trying to bring her around. Meanwhile, Drew calls Nat and Rachel, telling them what has happened.

"They're flying back right now," Drew says. "Your mom's coming too. Maybe you should head back to the beach house until we know more."

"I'm staying here," I insist.

And I do. I stay there while the doctors try to help Aunt Sookie, and I'm there when they take her onto the ward. She's awake right then, but obviously very weak, and I'm under strict instructions from a very stern looking nurse not to tire her out. We stay with her for maybe twenty minutes before she falls asleep right in front of us.

"After something like this, she's going to be very tired," the nurse says. "You should let her rest now. Come back later."

This time, I give in to it, heading back to the beach house. It feels almost like a strange place then, without Aunt Sookie there. Astor and Drew are there with me, but they're almost as worried as I am. They don't even spend their time arguing, the way I might have thought they would. They're both too busy making sure I'm okay. Astor leaves after a while to head back to his canyon house. I think he's realized there's nothing he can do here.

When Rachel, Nat and my mother arrive, I rush to hug each of them. How long has it been since I saw my mother? She looks a lot like Aunt Sookie, only a few years older, and with my coloring rather than hers. She's a little shorter than I am, and when she looks up at me as I hug her, I can see the worry there.

"How is she?" she asks.

I shake my head. "They think it's serious. They were talking about complications, and possible heart attacks, and…"

"Shh, it's going to be fine."

Rachel obviously doesn't believe that, because there are tears in her eyes as she stands next to Ryan. Nat doesn't look like he believes it either. There's so much to do in that next little while, working out who gets to go to the hospital, and trying to deal with things around the house.

In the end, Mom, Rachel, Nat, Drew and I all go to see Aunt Sookie together. She's sitting up in bed, but she doesn't look even close to being well. She talks to Mom for a while first, while the rest of us wait outside. Then, eventually, Mom tells us that we can go in. Aunt Sookie looks so pale that she's almost grey, and the monitors hooked up to her are a constant reminder of just how sick she is.

Even so, she manages to smile when we crowd around her bed, and hugs us one by one.

"Look at you. All of you. You've grown into such fine young people. I never had children. I guess I've never felt the need to have any, because the four of you have always felt like you're mine anyway. I'm so proud of all of you."

I can see tears starting to fall from her eyes, but Aunt Sookie wipes them away with the back of her hand. It seems so wrong that someone so young and full of life should suddenly be so sick.

She smiles then. "You know, without the four of you, I wouldn't have my acting academy. It was only when I was playing games with you as kids that I realized how much I enjoyed getting other people to do that kind of thing. You've given me some of the most special times."

She looks over at Nat. "Nat, you've always had the most responsibility, but you're turning into a good man, and I know that you'll be able to handle it. Just don't let handling life be the only thing. You're meant to enjoy it as well."

"Rachel." Aunt Sookie smiles over at her. "I'm glad you've found the courage to express yourself the way you want to, and I'm glad you've found someone who makes you happy. Just remember not to lose that sense of yourself in it all. Be yourself, and do what you think is right, or all the rest of it doesn't mean much."

She looks over to Drew next. "Now, Drew, you've changed so much from when you were a little boy. You've grown, and you obviously have different dreams. Just remember that boy, though, because sometimes, I think you'll find it helps to think of whether he'd be proud of what you're doing. And instead of worrying what others think of you, concentrate on what you care about instead."

"And Summer." Aunt Sookie's eyes meet mine. "My own flesh and blood, but it's always been about so much more than that. You remind me of your mother, you remind me of myself. But the truth is that you aren't either of us. You're you. Uniquely, wonderfully you, and I couldn't be a prouder aunt than I am right now."

I don't like this. It feels too much like my aunt is saying goodbye to us. "Aunt Sookie, why tell us all this? Pretty soon, you're going to be home, and none of this will matter."

Aunt Sookie shakes her head. "Listen to me, all of you. The doctors have told me how sick I am. I might be okay, that's true, but things... well, we have no way of knowing how things will work out. If something happens to me..."

"Nothing is going to happen to you," Nat insists.

Aunt Sookie takes his hand. "I hope not, but it might. And if something happens to me, then I want you all to be happy. I couldn't imagine anyone loving my home or my school the way the four of you do, which is why, if anything goes wrong, I'm giving the four of you the school. I think you could continue the summer program without me."

She looks at me again, smiling once more. "You'd get the beach house, Summer. I know it's a place you've always loved, and... well, it would be nice to know that you had a place of your own all paid for. I know it gave me a lot of freedom after the divorce."

We step out of the room to let Mom back in, and I see that Astor is there. He moves to hold me, and I let him, even though I can see Nat's eyes on me as he does it. Nat looks hurt, so hurt that I want to rush to him and hold him the way Astor's holding me. I can't though. Not now.

"How did it go?" Astor asks me.

I shake my head. "Aunt Sookie... she's talking like she's dying."

He holds me tighter then, and I can see that Drew has his arm around Rachel. They look more like twins than ever then, because their expressions of worried grief are almost identical. I know that things still aren't right between them. I know Rachel probably still thinks Drew is playing around with too many girls, and that Drew still doesn't quite trust Ryan. Even so, it's obvious in that moment just how much the two of them love one another. I get the feeling that, whatever's between them right then, the twins will work it out. I'm not so sure about Nat, though.

An alarm sounds from inside Aunt Sookie's room. Mom comes rushing out of the room, and doctors start rushing in.

"What's happening?" I ask.

Nat rushes forward to grab the arm of a doctor. "What's going on?"

"Ms. Jones has had a reaction to her medication. We have to deal with it now."

He brushes Nat off and heads into the room. In the chaos, Nat's arm touches mine, just briefly. It feels like electricity jumps between us. I know he feels it too, because I look up and our eyes meet. He reaches out for me, but Astor's arm is still around me, and Astor takes a step back, moving me away from Nat.

Nat looks at him and he's just so *angry*. He looks furious that Astor might dare to move me away from him. Or maybe he's just angry at this whole situation, and Astor is just a convenient target for it. The trouble is, when I look at Astor's expression, he looks just the same. He looks like he would happily fight Nat there and then if it weren't for the fact that they're both outside Aunt Sookie's hospital room.

"Don't," I say. "Just don't, both of you."

Nat nods, and then looks at me. "I can't stay here like this," he says. "Summer, if you need anything, you know you only have to ask."

He leaves then, and I can see Rachel's eyes following him accusingly. She obviously can't understand him walking out like that when Aunt Sookie is in so much danger. I think I can understand it, but my eyes follow him anyway. I watch him all the way down the hall. All the way to the exit.

Then he's gone, and we're left standing in a hallway, waiting for the doctors to come out. One of them finally does, and he looks grave as he explains to us that Aunt Sookie had a serious reaction to her medication, and that she's now in a lot of danger. Mom asks if we can go back in, and the doctor tells us that Aunt Sookie isn't awake just yet. Even when she is, it can't be any more than one of us.

So eventually, Mom goes in, while we're left outside, waiting to see what will happen next, and hoping that somehow, it won't be as bad as the doctors keep telling us. Eventually we all go back to the beach house.

Epilogue

Aunt Sookie dies in the night. Afterwards, the doctors explain that she suffered a massive heart attack as a result of complications from her diabetes, coupled with her adverse reaction to the medicine. The words go into me and then out again, barely registering.

Mom's there, so she takes care of most of the funeral arrangements, which will take place within the next few days, but I can't sit around in Aunt Sookie's house doing nothing. I just can't, because every time I do, I find memories coming back to me of times spent there with her. Every corner of her Malibu pad is filled with them. It's filled with *her*, and that hurts.

I guess the others feel the same way. Nat spends his time out on the beach, staring out over the ocean. Drew and Rachel spend their time together, and it's like someone has put a wall around them. I know I have to do something to help them, to help all of us deal with this. So I have an idea.

They aren't sure about it at first, but the more I talk to them about it, the more certain we all seem to be. My idea is a simple one, but it means that we aren't left with nothing to do, and it lets us say goodbye to Aunt Sookie in our own way. We arrange to hold the reception for the funeral in Aunt Sookie's school, and we make full use of the stage there, putting it to the use it was designed for, for once.

We put on a production of the Princess and the Pirate, with the four of us in our accustomed roles, the roles she assigned us the first day we met at Aunt Sookie's beach house. Only we do it with all the resources that the old theater has to offer, including a complete cast made up of almost all Sookie's old students. That includes Astor playing the role of the king. I'm sure it must seem strange to the few friends and family of Aunt Sookie who don't know the story, like her ex-husband, who I spot standing somewhere towards the back, but for most of us, it's simply what we need to do right then, to pass along Aunt Sookie's legacy through us and her students.

After that though… what? I head back to the beach house, telling my mom that there are still things I need to take care of there, and that I'll be back in time for school to re-start. I get the feeling that she's grateful for that, because it means that she can head back to be with Mrs. Donovan, helping her through the news that one of her closest friends has died. Almost as soon as I get back there, though, I know I've made a mistake.

The beach house is too empty. Drew, Nat and Rachel have all gone back to their home in San Francisco to deal with all the stuff that's waiting for them there; from their parents' postponed divorce to their mother's depression. My mom is with them. And I… I'm alone. Alone in a house where just about everything makes me want to cry, because it reminds me too much of my aunt.

And I still have a week of that left before summer vacation is over.

I'm still crying when the doorbell rings. It's Astor, dressed in muted colors and with a worried expression, but still looking as great as ever.

"What are you doing here?" I ask, and then correct myself. "I mean…"

Astor takes my hands and kisses them softly. "I know what you mean, Summer. It's all right."

I shake my head. "No, it isn't. I don't think it's ever going to be all right again."

He holds me tightly then. "You shouldn't be here. Not now. If you stay here, you'll come to hate it, and Sookie wouldn't want that. She'd want you to go on loving this place."

"Where else can I go?"

Astor has an answer to that, in the form of an extra ticket to North Carolina. "Come out there with me for the last week of summer. I'm shooting a lot, but at least we'll be together, and you won't be stuck here alone."

Loving Summer (Loving Summer Series #1)

I barely even have to think about it before I agree. I phone my mom to tell her where I'll be, pack a bag, and headed out with Astor before I can change my mind. I think it's about the best decision I could make. Astor's right. I don't want to end up hating Aunt Sookie's place. I don't want to start thinking about it just as the place where I was all alone after her death. I want it to stay that magical place where we spent so many summers, and right now, that means being somewhere else.

It means being out in North Carolina with Astor. The film crew doesn't mind that, because they're used to me by now. Lindsay New even comes up to talk to me a couple of times without Astor around. She's sweeter than I thought she'd be, and she's very kind about Aunt Sookie. It turns out that she lost her mom when she was a kid, so she kind of understands.

Even so, I find myself missing the others, despite Astor's best efforts to distract me. Even when he takes a day off to go hiking with me through the North Carolina country, I find myself thinking about how Drew, Nat and Rachel will be feeling. Just thinking about them makes something tighten sharply in my chest, and that makes me feel a small flash of fear in turn, because I'm almost paranoid about my health now, afraid of everything. If Aunt Sookie could die that young, *anybody* can.

When we get back from the hike, there's a letter waiting for me. It's obviously been around several places, and the last address, for the film shoot here, is in my mother's handwriting. There's a brief note from her in the envelope too, explaining that Aunt Sookie sent this a few days before her death, and that she'd forwarded it on because she thought I should read it. So I do.

Dear Summer, it reads, *I'm sending this because there are some things I wouldn't think of saying to you face to face. After all, you're a teenage girl, and I know how easy it is to embarrass one of those. I was one, after all.*

So I thought I'd put it down in writing just how much I've enjoyed having you here over the summer vacation. You and the Donovans. You've been such a positive influence on them this summer, working that natural magic of yours on them when they're around.

You've done them all a lot of good. Especially Drew and Nat.

I'll admit I was worried about Drew when he was younger. He always wanted so much attention, and at the start of the summer, I think that still came out a little, don't you?

I pause, thinking of all the girls he had around him, and find myself smiling. Aunt Sookie definitely has this part right. I keep reading.

Yet, with you there, he doesn't seem to be nearly so hung up on that anymore. You've clearly been a very good influence. Then there's Nat, of course. You may know how much pressure there is on him these days. His father wants him to run his company in the future. His mother... as much as I love Nadine, her current state of mind means that Nat has to help her with so many things. In theory, his father should be doing it, but theories rarely work out like that. Their marriage is not as strong as it might seem.

I shake my head. Aunt Sookie obviously mailed this before I found out about the divorce.

Then there's Rachel. Sometimes, I think it must be hardest for her, being the only girl. That's part of why I invited you all around. She needs you, and I think you need her too, Summer. As proud as I am of you, being an only child of a single mother, I think sometimes you do need the advice of a good friend. Now, you know how I am. I wasn't anticipating that. I thought this would just be one more glorious summer for all of us. I thought that my condition was nothing to worry about. Who knew that things would get quite so difficult? Still, maybe by the time you read this, my operation will have had the desired effect, and I'll be the old Aunt Sookie again (not that old, though).

I have to stop for a minute there, wiping away tears. It's a while before I can make myself continue reading.

Of course, it's also possible that things won't have gone so well. Whatever happens, I want you to know that I love you, and I love the Donovan children. It's the closest thing to a real family I've had. Who knows, maybe one day we will even be a family, because I know how much you love Nat, and I can see that you feel plenty for Drew too.

Loving Summer (Loving Summer Series #1)

I suspect that if you ever settle on either of them, they will be lucky young men. They can certainly use your influence in their lives. I know that Nat would benefit greatly by having you by his side when he finally takes over his father's company, while Drew... well, maybe you can help him to finally love himself the way you clearly do.

You're probably wondering why I haven't mentioned Astor at this point. You might even be taking it as evidence of my disapproval. That isn't quite true (and thankfully, you aren't Rachel, to do something just because someone disapproves). I think that Astor is a lovely boy, and a good student. I think that he will be even more successful as an actor than he currently is, and I think that is possibly the problem.

I have done the Hollywood marriage thing, darling, and it consumes everything. The work and the image take over until there isn't anything else left. You start out with someone you love, and quickly, you find that you're left with just their corporate brand, or their ego. You find that running away from the press gets old, and that no one is interested in you as a person. It is a lot to risk. And it takes someone really grounded to be able to handle that. Of course, it might be that Astor is just wonderful enough to be worth the risk, but I'm sure that Nat and Drew love you too.

I know that whatever you decide, you'll be happy, Summer, and that is the only thing I could ever wish. Whatever happens in the rest of this summer, whatever happens the rest of your life, it's important that you are happy, and stay that way. Even if things don't go the way I hope with my treatment, or if something else happens, remember that. We've had some wonderful times in the beach house over the years, and those are what I want you to take away with you. Not anything else.

Here's hoping that you get to make many more happy memories there yet.

Aunt Sookie.

I read that, and then read the whole message over again. It's so uniquely, totally, Aunt Sookie. I have to pause again partway through, but this time when I make it to the end, I very carefully fold up the paper. There's so much in there. Things that I'd like to think Aunt Sookie might have said to me one day, but like this, it's just as real. And she's right about one thing. I know I can't let this summer be the last happy summer we have at the beach house. Aunt Sookie would have wanted the summers with the Donovans and I to continue at the beach house…we're her children after all. We have to keep her school alive and her summer memories alive.

Although I'm in North Carolina with Astor, I get out my phone and text each one of the Donovans:

SEE YOU NEXT SUMMER OR SOONER.

Rachel: Sooner

Drew: Soon. Very soon. I miss you already.

Nat: Can't commit to a time, but I do want to see you again.

Kailin Gow

Summer, Drew, Nat, Rachel, and Astor's story continues in

Book 2 of the Loving Summer Series

Perfect Summer (Loving Summer Series #2)

February 2013

A Note from Kailin Gow

Thank you for reading Loving Summer. I hope you enjoyed it.

If you enjoyed it, I appreciate you letting others know. Positive reviews and word-of-mouth is very much appreciated, too. And you never know, if my publisher like your glowing review so much, you may find it quoted in the next Loving Summer book.

That's one of the best support any author can ask for!

I love hearing from my readers! You can reach me at:

booksbykailingow@gmail.com

Kailin Gow

Weigh in on LOVING SUMMER!

Which Team are You On? Who should
Summer End Up With? Weigh in and Help the
author decide:

Team Drew

Team Nat

Team Astor

Vote on theEDGEbooks.com's

Loving Summer Poll

If you enjoyed Loving Summer, you may enjoy Saving You Saving Me, too!

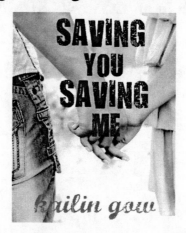

Aspiring psychiatrist Samantha Sullivan (Sam) never thought she would fall for the one mysterious guy she has been speaking to over the phone for months, the boy the counselors called Daggers. She wasn't supposed to talk to him outside of their sessions. But as she began to peel the layers of Daggers and learn who he is, the one boy she is supposed to be saving, might just be the one who is saving her. A YA-Mature romance from Kailin Gow with a real life tie-in to a community crisis help site inspired by this book.

OTHER BOOKS FROM KAILIN GOW

The FROST Series

The PULSE Series

Wicked Woods Series

Desire Series

Steampunk Scarlett Series

The Fire Wars Series

Fade Series

Circus of Curiosities

You & Me Trilogy

Never Say Never Series

Alchemists Academy Series

Loving Summer (Loving Summer Series #1)

Wordwick Games Series

Phantom Diaries Series

Beautiful Beings Series

Stoker Sisters Series

And More!

VISIT KAILIN'S WEBSITE to learn about new releases, the most awesome contests and parties, what Kailin and friends are doing in the community, workshops and events Kailin will be at and more at:

http://www.KailinGowBooks.com

http://kailingow.wordpress.com

and

on Twitter at: @kailingow

CPSIA information can be obtained at www.ICGtesting.com
Printed in the USA
LVOW131702140613

338654LV00003B/347/P